This is a work of fiction. All of the characters, names, incidents, organizations and dialogue in this novel are either the products of the author's imagination or used fictitiously. Any resemblance to actual persons, living or dead, or actual events is entirely coincidental.

Devious: Tiffany's Story
Eureka Johnson

Interact with the Author:
authoreurekajohnson@gmail.com
on Twitter: @authoreurekajohnson
on Facebook: Eureka Johnson

ACKNOWLEDGEMENTS

I would like to thank everybody who took part in helping me put this book together. To my two favorite readers, my good friend/sister Diane and my oldest daughter Erika. Thank you guys. I know you both had to get tired of me sending you parts of this book every day. LOL I appreciated it way more than you ladies know and love you both for it. Thanks to my Jaylin, he was my go to guy, when I felt like I was getting carried away. He's not a reader but he's a great listener. Jaylin, thank you for always sitting through me talking your head off. You truly are my favorite son. All my friends are going to think that the characters in this story is them. NO, THEY ARE NOT! LISA P. THIS HAS NOTHING TO DO WITH YOU! This is ALL fictional. I love all my friends and hope that none of this ever happened between us. Our lives were pretty boring growing up. (Mine still is) I have to say thank to my

brother, Ray. He is like my twin born years later than me. We are always on the same page. I love you Ray, you inspire me so much. I love our six hour brother sister phone conversations. To my favorite girl in world, without you none of this would possible. Thank you Mommy, I love you. You are the best mother in the world. To my big head brother, Redd, you know we share a bond that is out of this world. I'm so grateful for that. We have instilled it in our kids. The poor things don't know if they cousins or sisters and brothers. And to my baby girl, Ivery. This book is for you. I hope I make plenty money so that I can hire somebody to drive you around to all the things you want to do, because mommy is tired, baby. And last but not least I would like to thank the love of my life. Its funny how and who you fall in love with. But I love you Rich. If I forgot anybody…sorry I love y'all too though.

Chapter

1

My name is Tiffany Jones-Robinson, people call me a know-it-all. I don't consider myself a know-it-all, I consider myself a seasoned woman, who has been through more than my fair share of men and fucked up situations. I've dealt with so many things that I consider myself an expert on life, but I don't know it all. If I did, I wouldn't be writing from this prison cell. I know you're wondering how I got here, right? Well, living a destructive, carefree life has landed me with two life sentences.

I grew up without a father. He overdosed on drugs when I was only three. That left me with my mother and older brother, Joe. My mother despised me. On the first day of kindergarten, she told me to get myself ready for school and my brother, who is only three years older than me, walk me to school. "Mommy, mommy, it's time for school," I said smiling. "Tiffany, if you don't get your ugly ass out of here I will kick your little black ass." my mom said while lying in bed. "But, I need my hair done and my clothes on." "Get the fuck out!!" mom said.

"Come on Tiff, I'll help you get ready for school," said Joe. "You can't do my hair." I said laughing as Joe tried. "Yes, I can. I can do it better than you." Joe said. "Well, hurry up Joe. I want to meet my new friends and teacher. I hope Michelle and Tanya are in my class, then I won't be scared," I said. "Tiffany, you're smarter than me and I can tie my own shoes, why would you be scared?" Joe asked. "Because, KiKi and Monique talk about me. They say my hair is always nappy and my clothes never match. I know my colors, Joe." I said and begin crying. "Stop, being so weepy. You cry so much people are going to beat you up. I'm not going to let them hurt Tiff, but you have to stop crying. You should have told me those girls were messing with you, I would have done my karate moves on them.

Now, come on we can't be late for school. Bye mom." Joe said. "Bye baby, see you after school." mom said.

That school year, I had too many fights after school. KiKi and Monique were cousins, Monique was the main one I fought. It seems like we would have been friends, seeing as though, we lived next door to each other. She was a biracial girl, who thought she was too cute. "Ugh, Tiffany your hair is so nappy. You look like you're poor." She said, being coached by Kiki. I didn't even reply with my mouth, I let my hands do the talking. I beat her ass so good, KiKi didn't even look my way, not that time anyway.

KiKi tried to fight in school, thinking somebody would help her or she would get a hit in before the teacher broke it up. I would never do that, I didn't let anything distract me while I was in school learning. Plus, my mom would have kicked my ass, now that's a fight I know I couldn't win. KiKi was scary, I beat her ass every time I felt like it. Which was almost every day after school. I had to get my frustrations out some way.

I was eight years old when I took over getting myself dressed and making sure my hair was decent. I didn't understand why my mom wouldn't do my hair and dress me pretty like the rest of the girls in my class. "Mommy, can you do my hair like Michelle's?" I asked. "Tiffany, why are you bothering me? Would you like to go live with your aunt in Florida? I wish you would, it would make both of our lives easier. What do you want to stay here for? Why did your daddy die and leave you with me? I told him, I was fine with having only one child." she said. I was crying.

"What are you crying for? Yeah, I want you to go live with your aunt. It doesn't make sense for me to sit here and lie." she said smirking. "Why? Joe wants me to stay here. He said he needs me to stay here." I said. "He's just talking. He don't give a shit if you stay or go. He only wants to play football with his friends. He's not thinking about you or me." she said and laughed harder.

At that, moment Joe walked in. "Why you crying, Tiffany? You need to stop crying, that's why people always pick on you. Stop crying and show them it doesn't bother you." Joe said. "I told her she should move to Florida with her aunt, then she wouldn't be bothering us with all that crying." said mom. "Mom, she doesn't bother us. All she ever does is read books. Plus, she's fun to play with. Come on, Tiffie lets go in the backyard." "Wait before you go outside Joe, I need to tell to you something." Mom said. "Okay." Joe said. "I'm getting married and having another baby. Tiffany, go get me some ice water." Mom said dryly. "Wow." Was the only word that came out of Joe's mouth.

I went to get my mom some ice water. I went to the kitchen to get a cup and pretended like I had to use the bathroom. I took my mom's cup in the bathroom and dipped it in the toilet and got some water, walked out the bathroom, went to the kitchen and got some ice, put it in the cup and took it to her. That made me feel better. I was laughing so hard, it took me a while to take her the water. I had to stand there and watch her drink it.

My mom was four months pregnant when she told Joe and me. She got married that following Friday night, and had Trey five months later. He was such a beautiful, peaceful baby, but here we were living with this man, Dave, we didn't even know. Joe didn't like him, but I did. He didn't let my mom be mean to me. Dave would buy me candy, come in my room and sit on my bed to talk to me. If my mom wasn't around, he would lay with his head in my lap. I didn't see anything wrong with it, although, Joe did. Joe used to tell me to stay away from him and if he ever touched me I have to let mommy know.

Trey was three months old the first time his dad touched me, he was six years old the last time his dad touched me. At first, Dave just started off kissing me. I didn't think anything was wrong with it, when he put his hand in my panties, I knew something was wrong. I told him to stop or I was going to tell my mom. He stopped, took his belt off and beat my ass like I had stolen something. That was the last time I used that threat. I let him touch me, even though it felt gross, I preferred that over an ass beating.

He would come in my room in the middle of the night, slip his hand in the side of my panties and whisper in my ear, if I screamed will beat me. I let him do it, hoping my mother or brother would wake up and help me. One night, he almost got caught in the act. "Dave, why are you standing over Tiffany's bed?" mom said. He looked like a dear caught in headlights, not able to think of a lie quickly enough. "I said what the fuck are you doing standing over that girl's bed?" mom said again this time not so patiently. "Nothing, I thought I heard her talking on the phone." he said nervously. "That don't make sense. Who the fuck would she be calling at 3:30 in the morning? You know what fuck it. Get the fuck out of there before you wake her up." Mom said.

"Girl, I still have an eerie feeling about him standing over Tiffany's bed like that. I don't want to ask her if he has touched her or not. I don't want to plant ideas in her head. If he was she would tell Joe and he can't hold water so I know he would told me." My mom said. She was on the phone whispering, not knowing I could hear her. I wanted to walk in the room and tell her. I was afraid she wouldn't believe me and would think I was nasty for letting him put his hands in my panties. She continued, "I'll tell you like this, if I ever find out he's touching her, I'm going to shoot his balls smooth off his body. You're laughing girl, I'm serious as hell. One thing I don't like is an adult who take advantage of kids." After that night, he didn't come back in my room for a month.

My mother watched him like crazy. Once he thought she let her guard down, it all started again. He became very bold, he would touch me when I walked past him, or kiss me when my mom was in the other room on the phone. One time, he was tried to kiss me and Joe walked in, he pushed me, I fell, he tried to act like I was clumsy and he was helping me up. Joe didn't think anything of it. I wish he would have because Dave's kissing and touching went on for too long.

I left for Florida the same day school got out, my eighth grade year, and I came back one week before school started, my ninth grade year. That was the best summer of my life. I loved my aunt and wished I would've chosen to live with her when I was younger. It's too late now, I had all my friends at home. Plus my brother, Joe had become my best friend and I couldn't leave my best friend. He did everything for me. I could talk to him about things that bothered me. Nobody else understood the pain in heart. When I got back home nobody could believe their eyes, especially Dave.

When I left I had a little girl's body, when I returned I had a grown woman's body. My breast were a very full C cup, you could see my nipples through my shirt. I had gone up two whole pant sizes because of my thighs and butt. My waist was very small, my legs were big, shapely, and pretty. That was the first time my mom ever told me I was cute. I had on some mid-thigh length blue jean shorts, a red halter belly top and some red sandals. I asked my mom if I could cut my hair, she said yes. My aunt took me to the salon to get it cut and she took me to get it styled once a week.

My aunt had taken me school shopping before I went home. I loved all my stuff because I got to pick it. She bought me everything I wanted including jewelry. I'd never had a necklace, hoop earrings, or a bracelet before. I thought I was the bomb.com! While I was to showing off my jewels, Dave was watching my body. He was almost salivating. I was too busy flashing my bling in Joe's face to notice, but my mom did and didn't say a word.

Later that night, my mom said she would rent movies and get snacks for my brothers and me. They were running out while I was in the shower and would be right back. I was putting on my pajamas, when Dave just burst into my room. I tried to hurry up and put my clothes on. Dave grabbed my shirt and threw me down on the bed, he was trying to suck my breast, but I was putting up a good fight, so he couldn't. He slapped the dog shit out of me.

WHAT?? This nigga don't know what he just did. I was an

angry, mistreated, 5'10" 125 lbs. child, whose brothers took

karate classes and taught her everything they learned. Once

I got over the initial shock, he touched my leg and I kicked

him dead in the nose. Blood was squirting everywhere. I

didn't stop there, I karate chopped him in the throat and

kicked him in the balls. I grabbed my clothes and ran

outside to wait on my mom.

"Tiffany, what are you doing out here in your night

clothes?" mom said. "That man tried to rape me." "What

man?" mom said. "Your husband!" "Oh yeah?" I answered

yes and told her what happened. She told me to go back

and in the house and don't say shit because she had a plan.

I was confused. I thought she really had no love for me. I

was disappointed, this was not the time to plan shit. I knew

Dave was going to rape me for sure. I turned around to

walk toward the house, she stopped me, said act normal, kissed me on the cheek and told me she loved me. I started to cry. This time it was tears of joy, something I had never experience. At that moment I trusted my mom. She told me her plan and I went back in the house.

I went to my room. Dave ripped the bloody sheets off my day bed and was in the shower. When he got out I was putting new sheets on my bed. "Did your mother come back yet?" he said. "Yes, but I told her I was hungry, she said was going to get pizza." I said not looking at him. He came closer and grabbed me by my shoulders and lifted my head. "Did you tell her anything?" he said. "No." He dropped his towel, I made a dash for my bedroom door and made it by an inch. I ran for the front door, as I was opening it, he tackled me and I fell. I kicked him in the gut, which got him off of me long enough for me to make it outside.

I made it outside to the bush where my mom was waiting and nodded my head. She took off running in the house, with me and my brothers hot on her trail. "Oh, so you like to rape little girls, now do you?" mom said while digging in her purse. My brothers and I knew what that meant. We all looked at each other and jumped on the floor. As soon as we got down on the floor, three shots rang out. Two hit the wall and one hit Dave right in the balls. Now, that's love. If I never knew my mom loved me that night, she proved it.

My mom took out a cigarette and lighter, sat down on the couch and asked Trey for the remote control to the TV. I sat down next to her and put my head on her shoulder. "Joe, call the police and tell them this motherfucker is over there bleeding all over my gotdamn floor!" "I don't even put my own damn hands on my kids, I know fucking well ain't no man about too....And rape my daughter in the house her daddy bought? How long has this shit been going on, Tiffany?" Mom said puffing on her cigarette. "Six years." I said feeling ashamed and dirty; however, I refused to cry. "Six years? I should have never married you, you nasty ass nigga! I knew some shit was going on. There's no reason for a grown man to be standing over a little girl's bed." mom said. She jumped to her feet, ran over and kicked Dave in his almost non-existent balls. He yelped out in pain. By then the police were arriving.

My mom sat there like she hadn't done a thing. When the police came in and saw Dave they stopped in their tracks, looked at my mom and asked what happened. "This sick bastard was trying to rape my daughter, I didn't think he needed his balls anymore. It's obvious he has a pair somewhere else that are bigger, because he tried to rape her while I went to the corner store." my mom said. "Get this piece of shit out of here. Tell me what happened young lady, start with your name and age." the short officer said.

"Tiffany Diane Jones and I'm fourteen years old. I'd just gotten out the shower, and went into my room. He came bursting through the door. I tried to hurry up and put my clothes on, but he was quick. He grabbed me and tried to ummm…ummmm put his mouth on my breast, but he couldn't because I kept moving. When he touched my leg, I used my karate moves and kicked him in the nose, then I karate chopped him in the throat and kicked him in the balls." I said calmly.

The whole room grew quiet, then erupted in laughter. "You got your ass whipped by a girl and then got shot by her mama?" the paramedic said. He was laughing, suddenly, his face turned to stone as he applied too much pressure to Dave's balls. "I told you to get this piece of shit out of here!" the short officer said. After that night, I agreed if I never had to see Dave again, I would be fine. If I

21

didn't, he would have pressed charges against my mom. She would have surely gotten time, her gun was not registered to her. She bought it from a guy in the hood.

While I was in Florida, I sent my mother pictures. She noticed my clothes were getting too small, she called my aunt and told her to get me new clothes. My aunt went without hesitation. She told me she had a feeling something wasn't right with Dave. Every time she mentioned him I would get tense, walk away and play with my cousin. She let me know it was okay to tell her if something was wrong; however, I didn't, I thought my mom would be extremely mad.

I didn't think my mom would believe me but, when I told my aunt about the situation, she told me she talked to my mom before I came home. She said my mom put the pictures I sent her in the bible, when she went back for them they were gone. She didn't think much of it, thought she misplaced them. A few days later, my mom heard moaning coming from the bathroom. The door was cracked, she crept up to it and peeked in. She saw Dave with my pictures spread out across the vanity, dick in hand jacking off. My mom was disgusted, nonetheless, she kept quiet and came up with 'the plan'.

Soon, things went back to normal. My mom and I still had a love/hate relationship. All she did was smoke cigarettes and talk on the phone all day. To this day, I hate the smell of cigarettes. Shortly after the incident, we talked. She told me she didn't hate me, she really missed my dad and I was a constant reminder of her lost love. I still felt so unloved and unwanted. I felt as though my daddy left me and my mom just didn't want me. If it wasn't for my brothers, I wouldn't know love at all, especially Joe, but, in the end he left me too.

My brother, Joe, was my Savior. He was there for me when I was feeling down. He always knew how to make me feel better, when my mom was making me feel like a piece of shit. He was everything to me. My sophomore year in high school, Joe dropped a bomb on me. He told me he was moving to California with a girl he'd met. I didn't believe him. Of all people, I knew Joe wouldn't leave me, but he left and went to California. We talked on the phone every other day, for twenty minutes. I tried not to let the distance break our bond. Eventually, it did, totally. I didn't trust him anymore. I loved him to death and I was very sad our lives went in different directions.

Chapter

2

My teenage years started off great, socially. I was still having problems with my mom. After Joe left, I started talking back to my mom. Although, I was scared of her, I know she had to be scared of me too. She saw herself in me and that probably scared the shit out of her. I had to learn the hard way, she wasn't afraid of me.

She'd let me get away with saying little smart shit for a long time, since I was trying to deal with what happened to me. She was actually a tad bit more understanding than usual. I knew it was guilt. I don't know why, in my opinion, she did better than him going to jail. She became overprotective.

She wanted to me stay close to home so she started going to school. She paid me to watch Trey in the beginning. I didn't want to. I figured, if she would have went back to school when we were younger, I would have my time to be a teenager. When she first started school and was paying me, I was fine watching Trey, he was such a good boy. When she stopped paying me, I would leave him with my neighbor. She was an older lady, who loved cute little Trey. He liked her too, because she had big boobs.

My mom came home early one day so I could go to a party. I didn't know she was coming home. She told me I couldn't go to the party, I accepted it and moved on. Trey was at the neighbor's house and I was gone. She rode around the neighborhood until she found me.

"You bitch! Why did you leave Trey across the street? I told you to watch him. You know all too well what people are capable of. Don't you, Tiffany? Why would you put your brother at risk?" she said. I wanted her to shut the fuck up. I hadn't told anybody what happened for real. "Who you calling a bitch? " I said. "You're the bitch. I don't have kids, so you can't get mad I got somebody to do yo' ass a favor. Bitch please." That's all I remember until I woke up to all my friends standing around laughing at me.

They told me she whooped my ass like I needed it to be whooped. In the hood, it's very disrespectful to curse at your parents. After she knocked me the fuck out, she told my friends to tell me when I wake up get my ass home. I was so fucking scared. I didn't waste any time getting home. What the fuck had I done? I had to find a way to make this shit right. I walked in the house and burst into tears, saying how sorry I was and I would never ever try her again. I didn't. Lesson learned; however, every now and then I did add a laxative to her food, just to make myself feel better.

After that ass whooping, I changed towards my mom. She was right, I did put my little brother at risk. I started helping out more around the house without being told. I went back to being the quiet girl I once was. My mom liked the fact I was close to home all the time. I wanted to be out with my friends, but, I had to wait for a few years. I had to start over building trust with my mom. I stayed quiet for the next year and a half. My senior year of high school was approaching. It was time to have some fun. I had been waiting for this for a long time. I had maintained all A's from my first day of school and been through enough drama, it was past time to have some fun with my friends.

I had plenty friends, both male and female. I wanted to do regular teenaged shit. I wanted to hang out with my girls, Brittany and Tracie, in the hood. My hood was not the real hood, but it was hood enough for me. We were three bad bitches. I was always the tallest of my group of friends. I hadn't changed much physically.

I was still the same height, I now weighed 165 lbs. and had 36 DDD perky breast, a 28 inch waist and legs and thighs any grown woman would have died to have. I was fine. I still had my beautiful face and my short hair stayed fly, thanks to my girl Tracie. She was the neighborhood hairstylist. She could hook you up for $25.

Brittany and I lived across the street from each other. Tracie was fairly new to the neighborhood. She was from the east side of Detroit and we were on the west, but she was real cool though. The first day we met we hit it off. "Hey Brittany, what's up girl?" I said. "Nothing Tiff. I was going to walk around the corner to my friend Tracie's house." "Who is Tracie?" "She just moved around the corner." "How did you meet her?" "I saw her in the store and her hair was so cute. I asked who did it and she said she did. Tiffany, her shit looked so professional. She said she would hook me up for $25." "Do what to it?" "A full head of weave, girl!" Brittany said. "Get the fuck out of here! Does she do braids?" "I don't know. Go around there with me and you can ask her." "Okay, Cool." I said. We walked around the corner to Tracie's house.

Tracie was three years younger than us. You couldn't tell though, she acted just as old, if not older. She was a 5'8", dark skinned beauty. She had wide hip and an ass you could sit a cup on, a small waist, and really small breast. She came from a broken home, like the rest of us. It was her mom, twin sisters and her two brothers. She could basically do whatever she wanted, whenever she wanted. She had a house full of girls, some we knew, and some we didn't. Brittany introduced us.

"Hi, Tracie. This is my girl Tiffany. Tiffany this Tracie." Brittany said. "Hey Tracie, what's up?" I said. "Nothing much." she said. "Don't be shy, girl. Did you really do your own hair?" I said. "Yeah, but its messed up now." she said. "No, it's not. It looks better than mine even when I just finish it. If you consider that old I would love to see what freshly done is like." I said. "You would let me do you hair? I haven't done short hair too much. I know I can do it though. Why don't you let me practice on you and I'll do your hair for free." she said. "Hell yeah, girl!" I said and gave her a high five. Brittany was pouting. "What's wrong with you, Britt Brat?" I said. I knew what was wrong. "How are you going to get your hair done for free, this is my hook up." she said. Tracie cut in. "Brittany, you said you wanted a weave. I told you I would do it for $25. That's not what I charge everybody else. Trust me, you got a good deal. If you feel some kind of way about it though, I will throw in the hair." she said smiling. Brittany and I smiled also. We were all cool after that.

Now, Brittany was my girl. She was considered the fat girl of the crew. I never saw her as fat. She was bigger than us, but that didn't make her fat. I hated when people said that about her. She was 5'7", light skinned with freckles, huge breasts and ass. She had the face of an angel, but was truly hell on wheels. She was a slut and didn't care who knew it. She would fuck anybody who paid her some attention. Her huge ass attracted all the guys, her 'I'll do anything for attention,' attitude ran them away. In the short time, we were really cool, I know she had at least twenty sexual partners. One time, she hooked a friend from school up with a guy, turned around and fucked him while he was talking on the phone with the girl. She was a real piece of work, however, I loved the shit out of her. Brittany and Tracie got into more trouble together, I wasn't foolish enough to do the shit they would.

Brittany went to a different high school than Tracie and I. So Tracie and I ended up becoming closer after a while. Tracie was very secretive, that's the only thing I didn't like about her. She fucked just as many neighborhood guys as Brittany but she would never tell, not even her best friends. I knew better than to mess with guys in the neighborhood. My brother was very popular, and would have killed me if he found out, even though he was thousands of miles away. I was sneaky and messed with guys outside of the hood.

I liked guys that had cars and money, therefore, I dated drug dealers. The fast life was awesome. The first guy I ever had sex with was a drug dealer, after we had sex, he bought me everything I wanted and some shit I didn't want. I pretended to have a job so my mom wouldn't know how I got all those things and so I could spend time with Corey. Corey was so handsome. He was light brown, 6'4" tall, 230 lbs. of lean muscle with a smile that melted my panties right off my body. We met at the mall, while I was hanging with Brittany and Tracie. Corey was with his cousins, Mike and Tone. Tone liked Brittany but Mike didn't like Tracie.

We used to go out on dates together, I was scared to be alone with Corey. Although, I was afraid to be alone with Corey, I was fine being alone with Mike. Mike was silly and fine. I know I shouldn't have given my virginity to Mike, but I know he wanted it. I was sitting on my porch when Mike rode down the street. I tried to turn my head and not make any eye contact, that didn't work. He stopped. "What's up, Tiff?" He said. He had a southern accent I loved. "Just sitting here bored out of my mind. What's up with you, Mike?" I said. "About to head to the crib. Wanna roll wit me?" He said. "Sure, let me get my purse." I said. We made small talk until we got to his apartment in Suburban Detroit.

His apartment was super nice. I was impressed. I took my shoes off at the door. "You don't have to take your shoes off Tiffany, not unless you want to." he said. "Dang, it's a habit. My mom's been making me do it my whole life. It kept me from a ton of scrubbing, it's not a bad thing." I said. "Wanna watch a movie? I have some over there." he said. He pointed to the corner.

I looked through them, I didn't see anything I wanted to watch. Instead, I turned on the radio and danced. Mike sat there and drank a beer, he wouldn't take his eyes off me. I felt warm and tingly inside. I was really feeling myself and grinded sexier. I'm glad I chose to wear a dress that fit like a glove. Mike was really liking this. He was licking his lips and grabbing his dick. I was getting excited.

I went over to Mike and started gyrating on his lap, I felt his hard dick through his pants. I thought I was going to die. I'd never felt a penis a day in my life and had only seen one, I didn't want to see. I wanted to fuck Mike. I never experienced that before, but I went with it.

"Mike, do you want to show me your room?"

Yea…yeah…I mean yes. Damn, you got a nigga stuttering

and shit. Take your dress off and dance for me." He said. I'm glad I wore the right panty and bra set. I dropped my dress and posed. I knew my body was banging. I turned around to let him get a better view. I bent over and gave his a show. It was worth the fifty twenty dollar bills he threw at me.

Mike grabbed my hand and led me to his room. I was starting to get nervous, I couldn't let him know. He took my bra off and almost lost his mind. He kept saying I had the prettiest titties he'd ever seen. He took my panties off and ate my box. I didn't know what to think.

I was feeling so good I got brave and took his shirt and pants off. He dropped his boxer and I gasped. He had an 11" monster! Now, I see exactly why they called it a pipe. I was nervous, but I played it cool. He laid me back on bed, I almost lost my breath.

He kissed my neck and sucked my boobs. "Damn, this shit feel good." I said moaning. He smiled looking up at me and asked me if I was ready. "Hell yeah." I said. I didn't mean it. When he entered me, I don't know who screamed louder him or me.

That was the most painful shit I'd ever felt. Once he got a rhythm going, I was in heaven. When he noticed I was relaxed and enjoying it he pulled out and ejaculated. That had to be a world record. I may have been a virgin, but I knew sex was supposed to last longer than that.

"Damn, Tiffany!" was all he said before he collapsed. I was so confused. I was hoping he was okay, then I heard him snoring. I sat up and looked at him like he was crazy. "Wake up, Mike. What you going to sleep for? You haven't done anything." I said. "What girl? You know I laid it down." he said and smiled. "Um yeah. You laid your ass down and went to sleep." "Girl please. I know I can fuck."

he said. "Okay. Take me home." "You don't wanna go for round two?" "Do you have it in you?" "Of course I do." he said. He laid me back down. I left his house hardly able to walk.

When I got back to the hood, Brittany's house was my first stop. I had to count all the money in my purse, which totaled $2600. I couldn't believe it, I had to open a bank account in the morning. He told me there was more to come if I gave it to him like that again.

He had no idea I was a virgin. I always knew I was going to be the bomb in bed. Moaning turned me on, both mine and his. His was really loud, it had me in a zone, that's when I felt really funny. I started to shake uncontrollably and liquid squirted out of me like a waterfall, literally. I had a new found love and it wasn't sex. It was money.

I stayed the night at Brittany's house, so she could take

to open a bank account, she had a car. I had my first

savings account and it had $2,000 in it. I was so excited. I

wanted to save up enough money to pay for college, I knew

how I would do it. If anybody wanted to have sex with me

they would have to pay. I would only fuck with niggas, I

knew had money. I gave Brittany a $100 and bought her an

outfit and shoes. She was happy as hell. We went to lunch.

I went home took a shower then a nap and call Corey.

Corey asked if I could come over his house. I told him

yes if would pay for a cab. I got to Corey's in less than an

hour. He was drinking a beer, watching a movie. He

hugged me so tightly I couldn't breathe. "Stop it, Corey I

can't breathe, dummy." I said laughing. "I missed you

baby. Damn you smell good." "Thank you, Corey." "Come

here and give me my kisses, girl." "My pleasure." I said.

That night, I had sex with Corey, he only gave me $1500. I wasn't disappointed because I already knew Corey was cheap. I enjoyed the sex with Mike more than with Corey. For the next couple of months Mike and Corey had me gone. I had $60,000 in bank in that small amount of time, but my body was tired. I had to retire from that hustle and focus on getting a real job after graduation.

I had a dream about Mike. I dreamed he had been shot several times and was in the hospital. For some reason, I couldn't open the door to his hospital room, I pulled, kicked and scratched at the door and it still wouldn't open. Mike looked to be in a coma.

Suddenly, I heard machines beeping and doctors yelling. I knew that meant Mike died. But, instead he sat straight up, looked towards the door and said "I love you, Tiffany." When I woke up, I realized I was in love with

Mike. I had to cut ties with him, I was supposed to be in love with Corey, but I wasn't. I decided to let them both go.

I wasn't surprised Mike never told Corey about us. I told him if he wanted to keep seeing me he'd better not tell. He was sprung, he didn't tell. It was so easy and fun to have men wrapped around my fingers. They did it all the time, why couldn't women do it, too.

When I told the guys I was done with them, they took it better than I expected. Mike put up the most fuss. Corey acted like he didn't give a shit, but I saw him riding past my house all the time. I had to put my life back together, it was getting out of control.

I felt worse about letting Mike go than I did letting Corey go. Mike and I shared a connection. We talked about everything. He actually had plans of going back to school and becoming a lawyer one day. I believed him. He was so smart. When we talked, I felt the passion in his voice. He didn't want to sell drugs, it was the only way he had to support himself. Soon he would be stopping, so he could pursue his dreams. I was falling for Mike. I know I made the right choice when I stopped dealing with him. I couldn't stop thinking about him. I was in love. I needed a distraction, I needed my girls.

Tracie was the first one I called. She was more available than Brittany. I went over her house. She was acting weird and asking a ton of questions. I was wondering what she had been up to. I saw Tone, Brittany's boyfriend, coming out the basement. I asked what that was about. Of course, her secretive ass had a good excuse.

"He's helping clean out the basement right, Tone?" she said. "Yeah. What she said." he said and walked out the front door. It was some shit going on. This didn't feel right. I told Brittany, she said I always made shit up. I said okay and left that shit alone. Fuck it! If she didn't care, I didn't either.

I told Tracie everything, but she told me nothing. She had a miscarriage last month, the way I found out was she left the hospital papers on her dresser. I found out she was pregnant by Brittany's boyfriend, Tone. I'm not surprised.

When I saw Tone coming out of her basement, I got suspicious. I told Tracie to keep fucking Tone if she wanted too. He and Brittany weren't married, so no harm was being done. I told Brittany, I thought they had something going on. She didn't believe me until Tone told her it was true. That shit got messy real quick.

Brittany went to Tracie's house, pulled her out the door by her hair and beat the shit out of her. I had to get in the middle of these bitches. I tried to have them talk about their problems, but they weren't trying to hear me. I walked away before I beat both their asses. As I was walking away, I heard glass breaking.

Tracie was breaking the windows out of Brittany's car. I couldn't believe my eyes. Were these two girls were trying to kill each other over dick? I went back and pushed Tracie down on the ground and slapped the shit out of Brittany. "Now, y'all know better than this shit. Stop it right fucking now!" I said. They had surprised looks on their faces, like I was the one out there acting a fool. That's when Brittany told me I had to choose who I wanted to remain friends with. For some strange reason I chose Tracie.

Chapter

3

Tracie and I started going to parties meeting tons of guys. She had gotten really good at doing short hair, I looked like I just stepped out the salon every time we left the house. "Damn, Tiff, you're rocking those jeans girl." Tracie said. "Thank you, girl. My dress is cute with my shoes you're wearing. You can keep those." "Are you serious, Tiff? You told me these were your favorite shoes." "That was before I was introduced to Gucci. My feet are accustomed to the good shit now." I said.

Tracie had this look on her face, it worried me. It was a look of disgust or jealousy, they are so close to being the same I could hardly tell the difference. I blew it off. "Come on let's go, hater." I said.

There were so many people at the party, we didn't have to go inside to have fun. We were standing outside talking to some girls we knew from school, when this average looking guy approached us. I usually don't talk to average looking guys, but this guy had a good sense of humor. His name was Junior.

Junior smelled wonderful and was dressed to perfection. "Hi, how are you? My name is Junior and I was wondering if I could have a moment of your time, pretty lady?" Junior said. "I'm fine Junior. I'm Tiffany. It'll be my pleasure to give you a moment of my time." I said. I was impressed with his choice of words.

"You smell good, Junior." I said. Thanks, Tee. You smell nice too. You don't mind if I call you Tee do you?" "No, Tee is fine. Actually, I like it." I said. "If you don't mind, let's go to my car and talk for a while. It's directly across the street." "Okay, let me tell my girl and I'll be right back." I said. I walked away making my booty bounce more. I told Tracie where we were going and headed back. Junior and I went and sat in his car.

"You look good, Tiffany. What do I have to do to be your man? Junior said. "Make sure I'm well taken care of and loved." I said being honest. I liked Junior, he was nice and after a few minutes of talking with him, he didn't seem so bad. We talked for about an hour, it felt like I was talking to an old friend instead of a guy I'd just met. I wanted to stay longer, but Tracie was ready to go, since we came together we felt we should leave together. I took Junior's phone number. He told me to call him as soon as I got home and I did.

"Hey, Junior, it's me, Tiffany. I'm just calling to let you know I made it home safely." "Thanks for letting me know, baby. You know it's still early. You feel like going to get something to eat with me?" "Sure. Where are we going?" "You choose Tee. Anything is okay with me." "Okay, let's grab some White Castle. I haven't had any in a long time." "Give me your address and I'll come get you."

he said. I gave it to him. When he came, I took him out a plate of the food my mom cooked. That way, I wouldn't have to leave the house and could still talk to him.

We did very little talking, we were all over each in no time. I hadn't ever felt this way about a guy, I liked Junior's average looking ass. Before I knew it we were in the back seat getting it on. It had only been days since I was last with Mike and Corey, but who cares I liked this nigga. That night was the first of many for Junior and me.

We became inseparable. I was falling in love with Junior fast, I mean really fast. We found ourselves talking about marriage. We used to hang out with Tracie and a few other friends from time to time.

I wanted Junior and Tracie to get to know each other since they were the most important people in my life at that time. Tracie's shorts and tops got extremely short when she knew I was bringing Junior around. I didn't notice it until I was talking to Junior and he wasn't listening to me, I wondered why.

When I looked up, I saw Tracie had decided she would bend over right in his face. She had on the tiniest shorts ever invented. I went and kicked that hoe in the ass, grabbed Junior's hand and left.

That was the last straw with Tracie. I knew she would sleep with Junior if given the chance, I ended the friendship before I killed her. My focus was on something else and that's my Junior. He was wonderful. I was so happy I met him.

Three months later I found out I was pregnant. I had no idea whose baby it was. I had slept with Mike, Corey, and Junior all within days of each other, all unprotected. I said fuck it and decided to tell Junior it was his baby since I wanted to be with him anyway.

He was so happy about the baby, honestly, I was too. My mother didn't take it too well. "Tiffany, I know you didn't go out and get pregnant. You should know better. Why would want to bring a baby into this world and you have nothing to offer it?" "Mom, I'm going to graduate and go to college and still become a doctor." I said.

"Girl please, you can give those dreams up. Go apply for welfare and be happy with your drug dealing man. One things for sure, before that baby comes you have to move out. Trey and I are moving to California with Joe and his wife." mom said. "When did Joe get married?" "He's been married for like six months." she said puffing on a cigarette, "I know. You were very busy and haven't been in touch with your brother." "Okay, mom, I don't want to hear that right now." "When do you want to hear it, Tiffany, since this is your world and you know-it-all? You have a month to find somewhere to go." she said and left the room.

I refused to cry, even though, this is not how this was supposed to happen. I didn't have anywhere to go. I was seventeen years old, in high school, with no job. I took out my bank book and looked through it. I had $65,000 in the bank now. I had to think about what I was going to do.

I grabbed the newspaper and thumbed through the classifieds, looking to purchase a house for me and my baby. I told Junior what my mom said. They never got along. He told me not to worry about it, I could move in with him. I didn't like that idea; however, what choice did I have?

I hated my mom and vowed once she moved I wouldn't have anything else to do with her. She would never to get to know her grandchild and neither would my brothers. Fuck family, if they could up and leave you when you needed them most, they didn't need to be a part of my life. I had my own family now and I was happy. I would never treat my baby the way my mother treated me. I promised myself at moment and I meant it.

The next weekend, I moved in with Junior. That's when the arguing and fighting started. We were from two different worlds and I could see that now. He thought I was his property and he could control me. He'd wait for me outside school. We would argue because I wanted to go with my friends after school, I would always give in and go home. His behavior was pissing me off. I thought things would be better after the baby was born, I was wrong.

I married Junior at the age of eighteen, my first child, Layla, was already three months. I thought I found the love of my life, I was wrong. He still remained controlling and I was miserable. I added tremendously to my savings, I was proud of myself.

I was saving for college. It had been three years and I hadn't applied to one single college. I had intentions on applying soon. I worked at a hospital in the medical office. I saw this as a step in the right direction. Junior was still involved with drugs, I didn't like it anymore, it was too dangerous.

I drove Junior's car to take Layla to a doctor appointment, when I came out the car door was open, the sound system had been stolen out. A note was left telling Junior next time it could be me or Layla. I was scared, I rushed home, running lights and stop signs, not caring. Junior was sleeping on the couch.

"Junior, wake up!" "What is Layla okay?" "Yes, she's fine now. Look at this." showing him the note. "What is this, Tiff?" "That's what I want to know." I said. He read the note and looked up at me. "Tiffany, I know who did this. Don't worry, I'll handle this."

I didn't want him to handle this. This is just one situation, what about next time? We might not be so lucky. "Junior," I said. I walked to the back. "I'm not doing this anymore. I'm leaving. Layla doesn't deserve this lifestyle. I was cool with it when it was just us, now she's here. Somebody has to be responsible for her." "I'm responsible for all three of us, Tiffany. You act like shit happens all the time. This is the first and last time this is happening, I told you that. If you want to leave, I'm not going to stop you but, you're not taking my daughter with you." he said.

I wasn't thinking about what Junior said. Layla and I were going to a hotel until I found us an apartment. I was feeling nauseous, I sat down on the bed, until the wave passed. I'd finished packing, and told Layla to get some toys, when Junior grabbed my arm.

"I told you you're not taking Layla. Did you think I was joking?" he said. "I don't care if you were joking or not. I'm not leaving my child here. That defeats the purpose of me leaving. If you want your family, you know what you have to do, Junior. I'm scared for us, you have to understand." I said. I was feeling nauseous again. "If you leave Tee, we're are done!" "Okay, Junior, I'm gone." I said.

Chapter

4

I stayed in a hotel for about a week before I found a nice, quiet, and affordable townhome in the southern suburbs of Detroit. It was only $850 a month and close to my job. It took me a week and $8,000 to decorate it how I wanted it. It had three bedrooms, with large walk in closets, the master bedroom had a bathroom.

There were three bathrooms in all. I decorated Layla's bedroom and bathroom with princess stuff, the one downstairs with basic browns and beiges. The living room set I picked is the one I always wanted. It was a black leather sectional with three recliners.

I bought four 32" TVs. One for my room, Layla's room, the guest and the living room. Layla and I were playing Go Fish, when there was a knock on the door, we were waiting on the cable guy. I opened the door and almost pissed on myself.

The cable guy was my true love, Mike. I was so happy to see him, I jumped into his arms. He hugged me and looked over towards the floor where Layla was playing, then back at me. "Come on in, Mike how are you doing?" I said. "Fine and yourself?" he said walking over to Layla, "Who is this beautiful young lady?" "My name is Layla and I'm three years old." Layla said.

"Hi Layla, my name is Mike and I'm here to fix your TV." "Okay, can you do my room first? Mommy said I'm a princess and princesses get whatever they want, if they are a good girl." "Yes, they do, Princess, why don't you show me your room and I'll see what I can do to make you happy." he said. I smiled, he looked so happy with Layla. I wonder could this be his child. No, Layla has a dad.

We walked upstairs to Layla's room. "Wow, Layla, your room is beautiful." "My mommy let me pick out my stuff." she said smiling. "She's so pretty, Tiffany. She looks just like you." "Thank you. That's my little princess." I said.

"I heard you were married but, I didn't believe someone got you to settle down." Mike said. "I wasn't that bad, was I?" "I won't say you were bad, you were very good." he said with a little smile. I was blushing. "Well, ladies, I have to get to work if you wanna watch TV tonight." he said. I showed him what he needed me too and he got started.

Mike still looked good and still had that southern accent. I felt the old feelings I had for Mike resurfacing. I had to push them to the back, I was still married. I felt another wave of nausea come over me, this time, I had to vomit. I took off running to the bathroom and made it to the toilet just in time.

I vomited consistently for three minutes. I was wondering what could be wrong with me. Then it hit me, I hadn't had a period in two months. I felt nauseous again, this time for a different reason.

I know this can't be happening. I was starting to put my life together. I enrolled at the University of Michigan, classes started in two weeks. I was starting to feel hopeful about my future, now this. I hadn't talked to Junior in two and a half weeks. I had no intentions on it anytime soon, until now, I didn't have a choice.

How did this happen, I was on birth control. I called Junior, he answered on the first ring. "What? I told you it was over between us." he said. I heard a female voice in the back ground. "Who is that?" "I'm not your man, you gave up your right to know anything about me." he said.

I didn't feel like going through this with him. "I'm pregnant, Junior." I said. "What? Are you serious? Damn! This is not the time. Shit! Give me some time to process this. I'll call you later." he said and hung up the phone. I knew what that meant, give him some time to get rid of the chick at his crib.

I sat there in a daze. I didn't even hear Mike tell me he was done. He came over and tapped me on the shoulder. "What's up, Mike?" I said. "I'm all finished. Princess Layla is in her room watching cartoons. I need you to sign this and I will be out of your way." He continued.

"You look like you have a lot on your mind." "Yeah, I do have a lot on my mind." "Wanna talk about it?" he said. "What are you doing when you get off work tonight?" I said. "Nothing." "How about Layla and I cook dinner for you?" "Sure, sounds great. Where is your husband?" "We are no longer together." "Sorry to hear that, Tiff." he said. "Come over around 8. We will talk then." I said.

Layla and I went to CVS and Kroger. I had to get a pregnancy test and some more items for tonight. I was nervous about taking the pregnancy test. It's no way I needed another baby right now. I took the test and it was positive. I couldn't believe that shit.

I said fuck it, called and made a doctor appointment, and got ready to for Mike to come over. As always, Mike was on time. Layla greeted him at the door. "Hi Mike, my mommy told me you were her friend when was she was younger. Was she young a-cause she old now?" "Yes Princess, she was younger. She's not near old now, baby." he said. "Come on in Mike." I said.

"Puddin' Pop, take Mike's jacket and put it on the couch, then come and eat okay?" "Yes, mommy." Layla said. "Let's eat Mike." I said. The entire time we ate Mike talked to Layla and she listened intently. I smiled at the interaction. I know Layla missed Junior.

After dinner, the three of us cleaned up and ate ice cream. I told Layla to finish up and go upstairs, she did. "So, what's the story with you and your husband?" "I left him. I need to make sure Layla is safe. He's still selling drugs. He has no plans for the future. I don't want my children being raised around that." "Isn't Layla your only child?" "Yes, I had intentions on having more one day."

"You will. He will stop selling drugs when he is ready. He has to do it for him, not you, or Layla." "Well, you stopped. You had a plan years ago. He doesn't even have a plan. I haven't heard him say anything about a better life." "Everyone is not the same. I wanted out of that life. I'm almost done with law school. I have always wanted to be a lawyer, it was my own choice. If you love him give him time." Mike said.

"That's just it Mike, I don't love him enough to give him anymore of my time. I have dreams too. I registered for college, I have already wasted three years. I'm not waiting any longer. I don't want to talk about it anymore, I'm getting frustrated." I said.

We talked for two hours. He has so much going on in his life. He's in school, he's working for the cable company and he's single. I can't believe he's single. He said he's single because he needs to stay focused. Being in a relationship right now is not fair to a woman. That night and many nights after, Mike was in my bed. I missed him, he was my homie, lover, friend, and I valued that. After about two weeks of us sexing each other crazy, I told him I was pregnant and he convinced me to talk to Junior about.

I hadn't talked to Junior since I told him I was pregnant. He called a thousand times but I ignored him. Then, the day before my second prenatal visit, I called him.

"Hey Junior, how are you?" "I'm fine Tiffany. I've been calling you. Why are you just now returning my calls? I wanted to check on you and Layla." Junior said.

"I needed time to think, Junior. I have a doctor appointment tomorrow, if you would like to come with me. I'm 11 weeks pregnant. We need to talk about our future." "I agree, we do. I'm going to stop selling drugs. I want to be a father to my children and a good husband to you. I'm not saying this is going to happen overnight, but before the baby comes, I will have a regular nine to five. I promise." "Okay, Junior. Seeing is believing." I said.

Junior and I talked things through and got back together. We decided not to live in the same house. I refused to live with him as long as he was selling drugs. I started school and it was going great. Junior came to my townhouse to watch Layla while I went to school. Things were going good until my third trimester of pregnancy.

That's when bitches started calling me and telling me they were sleeping with Junior and all kinds of other shit.

The main one calling was this chick named Keisha. She was really ghetto. She told me she had been to my house and in my car. For some strange reason I didn't believe her. I figured she was saying that to get under my skin. It wasn't working.

Junior said he was changing for the better and wouldn't jeopardize what we had for some little skank. Keisha decided to give me the layout of my crib, even the baby's room. This baby couldn't come fast enough.

I was pissed. Here I was trying to better myself, Junior wasn't taking any steps to better himself like he was supposed to be doing. He wanted me to be in the house at all times. He dropped me off and picked me up from school, like I was his daughter, while he was out doing whatever in the hell he wanted to do.

He taught Layla how to dial his number in case I had anybody over. Layla, being the baby she was, told him about our dinner with Mike and he had been over sleeping in my bed. I didn't want to make Layla out to be a liar, so I confessed to it. That was the first time Junior put his hands on me. He choked me until I saw stars. I thought that was only in cartoons, trust me, it's real.

I didn't put up a fight or shed a tear because I was pregnant, but abuse was not for me. I felt my blood pressure rising as he slapped me around, all I did was protect my unborn child, by blocking my stomach from his blows. He didn't stop beating me until he heard Layla's cries from behind him.

I didn't want her to witness this, but I was extremely grateful, she saved me. He told me to go in the bathroom and clean myself up. He would take care of Layla. When I saw my face, it was red, my lips were busted, and I could see his fingerprints around my neck. I immediately became enraged, but willed myself to calm down, I would make him pay as soon as I had my baby.

The beatings went on until I was six weeks postpartum. They were getting worse. The University offered self-defense classes, I enrolled in them for the strength training and to help me drop the baby weight. I loved my son and so did Layla. She thought he was a baby doll. I named him Malik. I loved my children so much, I couldn't stay in this unhealthy relationship. I told Junior it was over. He said okay and left and didn't come back for three weeks. He wasn't helping me take care of our kids, but as long as I could maintain and didn't have to see him, my kids and I were fine.

Chapter

5

One night after I put the kids to bed, I looked at myself in the mirror and didn't like what I saw. I needed to get my hair and nails done. I needed a makeover. The next day, I called off work, took the kids to day care and got myself a complete makeover. I went shopping.

I felt good about myself, I was almost back down to my normal size, but with the way my body had taken a different shape, I didn't know if I want to lose any more weight. I liked my new body. I looked good in my new clothes. I decided I would take a break from shopping and sit down and have lunch. I looked across the food court and saw Mike.

I was surprised to see him, I hadn't seen him since he convinced me to talk to Junior about my pregnancy. I walked over to him, he was just as surprised to see me. We hugged then he introduced me to his fiancé. My heart sank to my feet, I couldn't believe he was getting married. I was jealous, while, I had no right to be. Mike was my true love. I had to think of a way to get him back. I played it cool, like I was happy for him. I wished him well and told him to give his number so we could keep in touch, he did.

Mike is the one person in my life I would never do anything bad to. I felt like he cared about me and had my best interest at heart. I did want him back, but I wanted him for good, that meant I had to clean up this mess of a life I had with Junior.

I would never do anything bad to Mike, but his fiancé is another story. When I get a divorce, her days with Mike were numbered. It was time for me to pick the children up from day care, go home and start dinner.

When I got to the day care I was in for a shock. The assistant told me my husband picked the children up. I started to panic. I never gave Junior permission to pick up the kids. Where had he taken my kids? "I never gave permission for anyone other than myself to pick up my kids. Why would you let someone you don't even know get them?" I said.

"He came in here with his picture I.D. and original birth certificates for them both. You never said you were going through a custody battle or anything. He is their father. He said you told him to get them, that's why he brought the documentation." the assistant said. "Did he say where they were going or anything?" "No." she said. "Thank You." I said. I left out slamming the door behind me.

I went straight to Junior's house. It was dark and there were no cars in the driveway. I got out and knocked anyway. No answer. I was furious and scared at the same time. Then it hit me. He had taken them to his mother's house, he didn't think I would act a fool over there.

He was wrong. I got to his mother's house in ten minutes. I jumped out the car and started walking toward the house when his sister, Laquisha, stopped me. "Don't come over here with no drama. Junior told us you have been keeping Layla and Malik from him. I dare you to try to keep them from me." Laquisha said. I was fuming.

Before she could say another word, I hit her in the mouth with all the strength I had. Blood was gushing out of the spot where here two front teeth used to sit. I didn't stop there, I grabbed her by her hair and kept punching her in the face. She was screaming so loud, before I could do anymore damage to her, Junior came running outside and pulled me off of her.

He punched me in the face and grabbed me by my neck. Something inside me snapped. I brought my knee up to his nuts with all my might. He doubled over in pain.

When he did, I gave that nigga an uppercut Mohammed Ali would have been proud of.

I ran in the house to find my kids. Layla was sitting on the floor playing with Malik. I told her to grab her things. I grabbed Malik's things and headed for the door. His mother came out the back and asked me what was going on, I told her. She told me don't step a foot in her house again. That was fine, I didn't like that fake bitch anyway. On my way out I made sure to knock over the bookshelf with all the family photos on it. I put my kids safely in their car seats and drove in a welcomed silence.

I went straight to the police station. I filed a report about everything that happened that night. From that night on anything Junior did or said I made sure to call the police or go to the police station and make a report. I needed documentation in black and white for the shit I had planned. This nigga was not going to keep playing with me.

I started to get cool with the girl next door to me, Angela, so I would have a witness to Junior's madness.

Angela was a nerve wrecking person. I learned my lesson about trying to have female friends, therefore I didn't get too close to Angela. She was a wannabe. I don't like a woman who doesn't have her own identity. Everything I did, she did. She was too clingy and nosey.

She had one daughter, Shonnie, who was the ugliest, fattest, little bad monster I had ever seen. I didn't want Layla or Malik playing with her but I knew it was inevitable. If I wanted to use Angela as part of my plan, they would have to play with Ugly Fatty.

Angela witnessed me on the phone with who she assumed was Junior. I would cry and scream, although I wasn't talking to anyone. She fell for it. I made her think Junior was sitting outside our townhouses. He wasn't. She went with me to file a few false police reports.

I had more than enough evidence on Junior. Soon, I wouldn't have to deal with Junior or Angela and her ugly fat monster. While we were at the police station waiting, I saw a friend I used to go to school with, Camille. We were pretty decent friends in school. I went over and talked with her.

"Hey Camille, girl how you doing?" "Hey Tiffany, I'm good under the circumstances, I'm going through." "Who you telling. I'm trying to get rid of my husband, he's been harassing me and I'm sick of it." I said. "Yeah, well my husband beats my ass and I'm tired of it. This is not how I expected it to be. I'm scared all the time, I don't know who he's going to be from one minute to the next." "Girl, I know the feeling." I said. My heart went out to Camille, I have always known her to be a sweet person. She didn't deserve this. I had to help her. I asked for her number so we could keep in touch.

I kept doing things to make Junior mad with me. He kept coming over and acting a fool. I would call Angela every time to make sure she witnessed it. After Junior left I would call the police. Angela would be right there putting her two cents in. I loved how naïve, Angela's dumb ass was. She wanted to be like me so much she went along with anything I said, even if she knew it wasn't any truth to it. I started going to lunch with Camille. We worked in the same vicinity, so it was easy for us to meet.

She was really going through a lot. She married a man fourteen years older than her. He had custody of his four children plus, they had two children together. She was taking care of all the children, while he did whatever he wanted to do. He would beat her if something didn't go right in his life.

He didn't have a job, she paid all the bills in the house. She was struggling really badly. Compared to her, my life was peachy. He was cheating on her. She had found him with numerous women in their home. I found out Camille was very weak and could easily be controlled.

I liked Camille and decided at that moment, if she was going to be controlled it would be by me. I had her best interest at heart. After work one night, I convinced Camille to go to a bar with me. We met some nice guys there. I convinced Camille to come with me and the guy I had just met to a hotel.

We got one room with two beds and got our groove on. I didn't even know the guy name I was fucking and I didn't care. I was a woman with need. I had to get them taken care of. I had a habit of not using protection. It was something I was accustomed to.

I had never used a condom in my life. I was on birth control, which was all that mattered. I never heard of a person getting a STD antibiotics couldn't cure. We had a ball that night and decided we would do it again soon.

When I got home, I fed the kids and put them to bed. I had a lot on my mind, I needed to think. I poured myself a glass of wine and sat down to gather my thoughts. I wanted a divorce, but I knew Junior would contest it. I had to think of another way to get Junior out of my life permanently. I had to handle this the only way I knew how. Ghetto style.

The next morning I went and registered for a permit to carry a weapon. I took the classes I needed to take. Once I got my permit, I purchased a Beretta Nano. I went to a shooting range to perfect my shooting. It was fun, I really like the feel of the gun in my hand.

I had some people needed to know not to play with me. I hadn't heard from Junior in a little over two weeks. That was good. I had a family reunion coming up in Florida. My aunt said I could leave the kids with her for a couple weeks while I finished up school. That was great.

After the family reunion, I came back home alone. I called Junior. "I wanted to say I'm sorry, Tiff. I've been acting stupid lately. How are the kids?" "They are just fine, in Florida with my aunt so I can finish this semester of school. I have to study for final and stuff. I wanted to talk about us, if you're up to it. Why don't you come over?" I said. "Okay, I will be there in about an hour." "Okay, bye." I said. I had to put my plan into motion quickly. I went and put on some boy shorts and a tank top, I knew Junior would love to see me in that.

In exactly an hour Junior was at my door. He let himself in. "Hey Tiff, baby. Come and give me a hug." he said. I went and gave him a hug. He was all over me, I was all over him. His scent was intoxicating, I still loved it. He undressed me slowly. Taking in every curve my babies had given me. I saw his dick getting hard through his pants. I was extremely turned on.

"I want to have rough sex tonight, baby. Can you do that for me?" "Anything you want, Tee. This is your dick." "I like the way that sounds." I said. I got an instant attitude, he was standing in my face lying. Keisha popped in my mind. I had to get mine and get this plan into action.

We were sexing for two hours. I wanted to make sure I was completely satisfied. I was. "Damn, that was good. It's been a long time since you gave it to me like that, Tee." "I know, I've been giving it to somebody else like that. He was unavailable tonight, so I had to settle for you." I said.

"What? What the fuck did you say to me?" he said. "You heard me, Junior. Don't act like you didn't know I was fucking somebody. This is his pussy, too. I won't tell if you won't." I said. I could see the veins in his temples throbbing. He was really pissed off. He walked over to me with his fist balled up. Before he could hit me I slapped him with all my might.

He punched me in the face and I smiled. That infuriated him more. He started to choke me. I scratched at his face and hands trying to get them from around my neck. When he let go I ran over to the couch and sat down, he came over and began punching me again.

I started screaming for dramatic purposes, I reached in the couch and pulled out my Beretta and shot his ass in the shoulder. He was so surprised, he started to cry and fell over on the floor. I called Angela, told her to call 911 and tell them she heard screaming and a gunshot coming from my home. She did. I called and told them what happened.

With the paper trail I had at the police department, the shooting was ruled as self-defense and I wasn't charged with anything. Junior was going to be fine. I had no intentions on killing the father of my children, I had a message to deliver and I think he got it.

Earlier that day, I went out and paid a crack head to set fire to his mother's and sister home, I knew I would be with the police. The incident could not be traced back to me. I didn't know the crack head and wore a disguise when I met him to get him to do the job and to pay him. I was satisfied with my pay back for those fuckers.

Chapter

6

I finished my finals and kept having secret night rendezvous with strangers, so did Camille. At one point we were doing that shit two to three times a week. It had started to get old to me. I wanted some new adventures, but I know I couldn't have any as long as Camille was still married.

I had filed for divorce and it was going fine. Junior was all for divorcing me, he thought I was crazy. Camille told me she was pregnant, she had no idea by whom. She didn't believe in abortion and wanted to keep the baby. I explained to the dumb girl, there was no way she could keep the baby. She claimed she wasn't having sex with her husband, so how in the hell could she explain this miraculous conception?

I met her husband a few times and he didn't like me. He told Camille she shouldn't hang around me, I didn't have the look of a married woman. He was right. I was fine and I knew it. I had the look of a woman who knew what she wanted out of life and did whatever she had to do to get it. His real problem was he'd hit on me and I turned him down.

Because I dressed like a hoochie didn't mean I was one. If he had been my type and his money was right, I would have considered it, but he was fat and ugly. Not my type at all. I never told Camille, it wasn't worth it. For some strange reason she really loved that cheating dog.

Camille was thick in all the right places. She had a beautiful face like a model face. She dressed like the business professional that she was, all the time, even when we went on our escapades. She said she dressed like that to keep the peace in her relationship. I had to convince this idiot to divorce this man so we could really have fun.

I finally made Camille have and abortion, if her husband would beat for nothing, I'm sure he would kill her for something like a baby. After the abortion it was like a light bulb went off in her head. She asked me to help her file for divorce without her husband knowing. I had a plan.

I gave her a rundown of my plan and put it into motion. All she had to do was go with me to Florida to get my kids, I would do the rest. I went to the strip club, I knew her husband, Ken, frequented. I paid two strippers to take him back to his house, fuck him and video record it.

It worked like a charm, he fell for it without, a doubt in my mind. Camille was sad at first, but I told her it was for the best. If she wanted out of this marriage, this was the best way. When we came back from Florida, she started her divorce. After Ken saw the tapes and knew it had been presented to the lawyer, he packed his things and moved. He left her with all the kids, including his previous four.

In the law office, I saw another childhood friend Michelle. She too, was getting a divorce. She was absolutely gorgeous. She had a killer body only money could buy after all, she did have six kids. I had to give it to Michelle, she was bad as fuck. She had nice perky 34 DD's, a 25 inch waist and 55 inch hips and ass. She seemed very depressed about her divorce. I was happy about mine, Camille was getting happy about hers, now it was time for me to work my magic on getting Michelle happy about hers.

After we left the law office, we went to lunch. Michelle told us about her marital problems. She said her husband was abusive, she didn't want her six daughters to grow up and see her getting beat on all the time. Her girls were her everything. I liked that, because my two children were my world also.

We talked for over three hours and promised to help each other get over this hump in our lives. As time went on the three of became close. Michelle was still distant, so we gave her space. All our divorces became final about a year later. I couldn't have been happier.

Camille had adjusted but, Michelle was having a hard time with it. I couldn't worry about her right now, I had big things going on in my life. I had been given two promotions at work and finished my Bachelor's degree in two years. I was excited.

So, I decided to take my girls out for an evening of fun. We went out to a bar. Neither Michelle nor Camille we drinkers, but I was. I got drunk and didn't have to worry about how I was getting home because Camille would take me.

I lived twenty five miles from her, but she didn't mind. Michelle left early, she didn't want her daughters seeing her coming in all late. I had a great time, I decided it was time for me to get my girls to start drinking and living it up, like I was.

I considered Michelle a party pooper. Most of the time, Camille and I would leave her at home and let her sulk in her depression. Camille and I always had fun. I would invite her over so I would have a babysitter for my kids, while we went out, since she still had Ken's older children.

I would have drinks at my house and go to this comedy club, where we had become regulars. We had so much fun. I was actually enjoying my life. One night I told Camille to spend the night because her kids were sleeping she did. I took the long way home and could have sworn I was Junior's car parked in the parking lot around the corner from my home. I quickly dismissed the thought, he wasn't crazy enough to come messing with me after I shot his ass. I would do it again.

I tried to deal with Michelle, she needed a friend. She was really going through it. She didn't want a divorce but she didn't want to stay with a man who beat her. I tried to help her get over her ex but to no avail. I was getting sick of her and that depression bullshit. She was bringing my spirits down.

Unlike, Camille, Michelle couldn't be talked into doing anything I wanted her to do. She was very strong willed and that pissed me off. I tried for three years to pull her out of her funk, she wouldn't bulge. I left her alone.

Camille and I still hung out. I decided to go back to school to work on getting my Master's degree. I was starting to see less and less of my children. I went to work in the daytime, school in the evening and at night I was in some man's bed. I met this man named James, he was cool. I dated James exclusively for three years.

James and I met at a night club. While I was with Camille, who is now known as Honey, her alter ego. I didn't need an alter ego, I was who I was and I was fine with it. James was a handsome dude and who had a really big dick and a vicious tongue.

I was actually sprung on James. He did and said all the right things. James wasn't usually the type of guy I would have dated but he had a certain charm and the sex was off the chain. When I first met him he had a job, and a car. He lived with his mother, but since she was a single woman, he told me he stayed there to make sure she was okay.

I went with that. It wasn't my place to judge the relationship he had with his mom. I knew I didn't want to make a life with James. Two years into our relationship, I starting noticing things about him I didn't like. He had two kids he hardly took care of. He still lived at home with his mom.

He quit his job and didn't have a car. I was in an established position at a prestigious hospital. He wasn't on my level. The sex thing was getting old. He was an alcoholic, I knew it was because of how his life was turning out. I used to do nice things for him like give him money, keep him groomed and supply him with liquor. He used to ask to use my car, I would say yes, I didn't see any harm in it, he was my man. That's when the phone calls from Diamond started.

Diamond was James' ex-girlfriend from high school. They kept in touch over the years, from what Diamond told me they never stopped sleeping together. I was pissed because here I was taking care of this bum, he had the nerves to cheat on me with a bitch that looked like a man. Every time they were together after he left that bitch would call me.

"Hey bitch, this Diamond and your man ate my pussy and fucked me so good right in the back seat of your Benz." "Look Diamond, you need to stop calling me about a nigga who can't do shit for you but leave your panties wet. Now, if you want to share the bum for his sexual skills we can, but these phone calls are getting a little ridiculous." I said.

She sat there quiet for a moment and then said. "I don't want him. I want you to know that I have been in your SUV and he spends money on me I'm sure you give him." "Girl that shit is neither here nor there. I don't give anyone anything I can't afford to lose and if he wants to spend the $100 I gave him on you so be it. My bank account is not suffering. As far as you being in my car, I'm sure that will be the closest you will ever get to luxury so enjoy, but make this you last time calling me. If you call me and tell me this shit again you're going to be very sorry." I said. "Are you threatening me, Tiffany?" "Of course not, Diamond, I would never do such a thing. I'm promising you, I'm not the one you want to fuck with. With that being said, lose my number and forget my fucking name." I said and hung up the phone.

I was furious with James. How dare that bum ass nigga to put that skank in my SUV. I work hard for the shit I have. I try to be nice to the less fortunate and look what the loser does. I had to end it with James before I ended up doing something he will regret. I was now twenty eight years old and I was starting to want more out of life. I wanted a real relationship, not this bullshit with James. That dick kept me right where I was. I couldn't leave him alone.

James was starting to spend more time at my house. I wasn't feeling that shit because of my daughter. She was growing into a fine, little thick, chick like her mom and I wasn't going to risk letting a man do to her what Dave did to me. I had to shut this down quickly. James would leave clothes hanging in my closet and I would politely bag his shit up and take it to his mother's house. His mother's house was going into foreclosure and he needed somewhere to go and asked could me move in with me, while drinking the last of the Kool-Aid Layla made right before she went to school. I ignored him and went upstairs.

When Layla got home from school and noticed her Kool-Aid was missing, she was mad. Her being mad, pissed me off, and I told James it was over and I never wanted to see him again. I told him he should be with Diamond, they were meant to be together. She called me again the day before, after I told her not too. She told me she rode past my house to see if she could see me since she had never laid eyes on me. I didn't say anything but my mind was working overtime. If this bitch wanted to see me, she would really soon.

I looked Diamond's ass up. I found out this bitch lived in the city. She was a hood bitch and I knew I would have to bring it. I stalked her for a few days. I learned she worked at Wal-Mart, she got off at 2:30 a.m., and got home at 3 a.m. I sat outside her house until 2:55 a.m., I waited for her to pull up in her driveway and walk around back to go in the house. I busted her ass in the face with the butt of my Beretta. Then I gave her the ass whooping she had been asking for. After I was done giving that bitch what she wanted, I told her to take a good look at me, so she would know how I look next time she wanted to ride past my house and shit. She was hood, so I didn't have to worry about her calling the police. That was the last time I heard from Diamond.

James never asked me about what happened to Diamond. I later found out Diamond was not the only person he was creeping with he was also seeing a girl by the name of Shanice. She didn't pose a threat, I wanted him to see somebody so he could leave my ass alone. He needed to learn, also. I was too good to him for the entire time we were together and this bum wanted to cheat on me. Plus, he drank Layla's Kool-Aid, I had to show him don't play with me. One night I pulled up to his mother's house unannounced, he was sitting on the back deck with, who I assumed was Shanice. I simply walked back there slapped the shit out of him, when he got up like he was going to do something, I pulled out my Beretta and told that bitch ass nigga to sit the fuck down.

I pulled my pants down and told both of those no good as motherfucker's to kiss my ass. I meant that shit too. Shanice was hesitant about doing it, but when I flashed my Beretta her way, she was more than happy to kiss the blackest part of my ass and so was James. I felt satisfied. I told James, if I ever saw him or heard from him again, I wasn't going to be so fucking nice. He would see what my Beretta was all about.

Chapter

7

That was the last time I saw James. I missed his sex so much, I thought about calling him on many occasions, but I didn't want any problems. I started hanging tough with Camille, or Honey, should I call her. She was not the same person anymore. She was man crazy. She was fucking and sucking like it was her job. She had been fired from her job for sexually harassing her boss. She was going crazy. I had to bring her down a notch. If it was one thing I believed in it was keeping a job. I felt like you have to be able to maintain the lifestyle to which you were accustomed. Honey, always had a good paying job, but now she was doing telemarketing. I couldn't have that so I got her a job at the hospital where I worked. I didn't let anyone know I knew her in case she tried some stupid shit again. She ended up doing a great job and got a promotion to office manager within the first two years she was there. I felt like a proud mother.

I taught her how to keep her extracurricular activities outside of the work place. I had completed my Master's degree and got another promotion. I was now the Research and Development Manager at Beaumont hospital, one of the best in Michigan. I basically ran the entire place. I was only thirty years old. I was proud of myself. I was still living in the same townhome I moved in when I left Junior. It was time for me to invest in buying a house. Angela had moved years ago. I so happy.

I started looking for homes. I didn't have time to really look for myself, so I had to find a realtor. I searched online and came across Angela's name. I didn't know she was a realtor. I decided to give her a chance to see if she could find me a good deal. I called her, she acted so surprised and amused I started to hang up on the dizzy broad. She told me to come into her office so we could figure out what I wanted and she could start the search.

I went into her office on my lunch break from work. Her office was nice and spacious. She had pictures of her and Ugly Fatty, and a cute little boy, who looked to be three years old. He looked familiar. "I didn't know you had another baby, Angela. Congratulations." I said. She looked at the paper work and skipped the subject. That was fine with me I didn't want to be her friend anyway. I was telling her what I was looking for in a house, when in walks Junior. I jumped to my feet, ready to pull out my gun, when he told me to relax he was here to see his girl. "Who is your girl?" I said. "Angela. We have a son and we are getting married." Junior said. He turned the picture around so I could get a good look at it. "This is our son, Trevon. He's three. Isn't he cute?" Junior said. I knew he was being funny. I was pissed and felt betrayed, but I didn't let those two assholes know. "He's alright. He looks like Malik did when he was younger. Speaking of Malik, do you ever plan on seeing your children again? They stopped asking about you years ago, but since you playing daddy to these other misfits, why don't you play daddy to your real kids?" I said. "They know how to get in touch with me if they want me." He said. He walked out the door.

Angela sat there like she had seen a ghost. I got up and told her it was nothing she could do for me. I didn't want to do business with a person who would stab me in the back. She didn't say a word, she held her head down. I couldn't believe Junior had a baby with Angela. I wondered how they even hooked up. I was going to find out. Even after all the things she thought Junior put me through, I can't believe she would still hook up with him. I felt betrayed, not because I wanted to be with Junior, but because he would actually marry a bitch that use to live next door to me for years.

I had to think of a way to teach Angela bitch ass a lesson. Even though, I didn't consider her a friend, she didn't know that. As far as she knew we were friends. She broke the girlfriend code. She was going to learn the code was sacred. Until I put a plan in place, I had to find another realtor. That's when I found a guy by the name of Connor Phillips.

Connor was the most gorgeous white man I had ever seen in my life. I could see it all over his face that he thought the same about me. I gave him the list of things I wanted in a house and how much I wanted to spend and before I left his office, he had three places he wanted to show me. We went to the first place, it was too small. I also didn't like the fact there was a trailer park two blocks away. I made too much money to live near those surroundings. He thought that was funny but at the same time, he said he liked an observant woman. I took that as a flirtatious statement and started to flirt back.

We went to the next house. It was gorgeous, just what I wanted. It had five bedrooms, a library, an office and an Olympic size swimming pool in the back yard. The kitchen was beautiful. It sat on the most beautiful lot I had ever seen. The neighborhood was immaculate. He pulled out the statistics for the school system. I was sold. This was the house for me. I was so excited about the house I ran over and hugged and kissed Connor.

That kiss lead into both of us being naked in the kitchen on the counter top. He had a big dick, the whole white man, small penis, thing is a myth. It had to be at least twelve inches and the girth was off the charts. I thought he was going to hurt me. He started undressing me. He stopped at my tits and once again I was told I had the prettiest titties ever seen. He started sucking them. It felt so good, I let out a moan that could be heard all over the empty house.

He went down on me. That shit was awesome. I returned the favor. He pulled out a condom, although, I had never used a condom before, I slid it on with my mouth. That made him rock hard. He turned me around and entered me from the back. That was some amazing sex. I couldn't believe a white man had me squirting and moaning so loud. I told him to lay on the island that was in the kitchen. I rode his dick like it would be the last time I would ever have sex. He begged me not to stop, so I did. We moved from the island back to the counter. I was losing my mind. He was hitting my spot. I was about to explode. When I did, he did too. That was some good shit.

After the session with Connor, he told me he would go to the office and get the paper work started. He asked if he could take me to dinner, I said yes. He seemed like a nice guy. We decided to meet at Ruth's Chris Steak House. I had been here many times and absolutely loved it. He wasn't cheap by far and I liked that. We talked for what seemed like an eternity. He was very smart and knowledgeable about more than real estate. We talked about politics, business and family. That's when he told me he was married. I didn't care I wasn't trying to marry him or even be in a relationship with him. He was my realtor, whom I happen to have sex with, no biggie.

Of course he gave me the story of how he and his wife were going through problems. I really didn't give a shit. I let him know he didn't need to make any excuses for what happened. I wasn't the type to get my feelings caught up in a man just because we had sex. He looked relieved when I said that. He went on to tell me how he would like to see me again. "I would really like to see you again, Tiffany. I don't want you to think all I want from you is sex. I really think we can have a genuine friendship." Connor said.

"Connor, it's okay. As I told you, I'm not looking for a relationship. What we did was cool. We are two consenting adults. We can be friends, but I don't want you to get your feelings caught up in me. You have to remember you are married. I will respect your union and hope you do the same. Do we have a deal?" I said. "Deal." He said. We shook hands and talked about my new house. He told me he would talk the owners down on the price. He guaranteed me the house was mine. I was ecstatic.

I went home and told Layla and Malik about the house. Layla was now thirteen years old and Malik was nine. Malik was very happy, jumping all around, doing flips and singing. Layla was not as happy. "Mom, I don't want to move. I like it here. This is where all my friends are." "Layla, baby, you act we are moving out of state. We are moving thirty minutes away. You can see your friends anytime you want me too. I promise." I said. "They can come over, too?" "Yes, my Puddin' Pop they sure can. I will pick them up myself." "Thank you, mommy. You're the best." I loved when she said that to me. I knew she really meant it.

A few days later, I went into Connor's office and got started on the paper work. I was really happy with the deal he got for me. So happy, we had sex right in his office, with his secretary right outside the door. I went home and started packing right away. While I was downstairs looking through boxes, I found a video tape. I knew it wasn't mine, it had to be Junior's. I popped it in the player and was so shocked at what I saw I almost fainted. I watched the tape for hours.

The scene on the tape started off in my house, in my bedroom. There were candles strategically placed all around. R. Kelly's Bump and Grind started playing. On the screen appears my ex-friend Tracie. She was doing a strip tease, when another woman walks into the shot. It was my neighbor Angela. She and Tracie started kissing and touching all over each other. Tracie goes down on Angela for a long time. Once the girl on girl action is done, in pops Junior, in his birthday suit. The girls began kissing and sucking all over Junior. He looks like he's in heaven.

The tape goes on for over an hour in my house, in my bed. I was sickened. I knew Junior was a dog but, I thought he had boundaries. I didn't think he would have sex with a person he knew I once considered a good friend. It was all good though. I knew what needed to be done. Later that night, I pulled out my black sweat suit and jumped in my car and headed to the city. I rode past Tracie's house, trying to see if anyone was coming or going. I knew Tracie had given birth a week ago, so her company would be limited. I took out the bricks I picked up along the way and tossed them straight through her picture window. I did the same thing to her car. When she came running out the house, I beat her ass, I didn't give a shit she had just had a baby. She kept saying I didn't have a heart because it's winter and her baby was inside. I pulled out my Beretta and told her to shut the fuck up.

I felt better. Now, it was Angela's turn. She would feel it the worse. I would start working on her in morning. I needed to get some rest for work. I could hardly sleep, thinking of what I could do to pay Angela back. I had an idea. I would needed Camille for this one. The next morning I called Camille in her office to tell her what was going on. I also told her about the plan I cooking up. She jumped right on board. She got the information I needed on Angela and we decided to meet at our usual spot after work. I was excited.

When 5 p.m. hit, I was running to get to Camille's office. She had her coat on ready to go. We drove separately, and made it at the same time. We were seated and I ordered myself a dirty martini. Camille still didn't drink. I would have to work on changing that, first things first. She handed me the information on Ms. Angela Holton. I read it over and was satisfied with the contents. Now, I had to find a friend of mine and put the plan in motion.

Later that week, I went to find my old acquaintance. I purchased a large sum of drugs and a few guns from him. I had Camille make an appointment with Angela at her office to assure she wouldn't be home before I could plant the drugs and guns in her house. Once I was sure Camille had Angela at the office and my friend knew where Junior was. I walked into Angela's house, she has never been a person to secure her home. I put the drugs in the kid's closets and the guns under the mattress in her room. Saturday morning, I woke up and called Child Protective Services, anonymously, and reported the crime she was committing. Harboring drugs and guns for a known drug dealer.

I sat down the street and watched as Angela was taken out in handcuffs and her children were put into a social workers car. I was hoping Junior would be there, but no such luck. I called Connor to see if he could get away for a while, he told me his wife was out of town, and I could come over his house. I thought my new home was fantastic, his shit was a mini mansion. It was decorated to perfection. He gave me a tour, and fixed me dinner. After dinner we had a few drinks, we had sex throughout the entire house. I ended up falling asleep, when I woke up Connor was lying there staring at me. "Connor, why are you staring at me?" "You're very beautiful when you're sleeping. I was admiring your beauty." "You're so sweet, but that shit is creepy, so don't do it again." I said. We both laughed.

"Yeah," he said, "I've been known to be a creepy dude."

We said our salutations and I left to go home. When I got home, Layla had packed up the kitchen, and her room and was helping Malik. I was proud of my Layla. She was a helpful person and I loved that about her. She asked me if I needed any help with my room, I told her no I could do it and she smiled and went back to helping Malik. I started packing up my room, we only had a week before we moved. I'd been really slacking. I needed to get back on my shit. We made our deadline and moved into our new home. We were all excited.

The kids loved the house more than I thought they would. Since it was winter time we didn't see any neighbors, I hoped it stayed that way because I didn't like neighbors. Two weeks after we moved Junior called me to tell me about what happened with Angela. "Hey Tiffany, are you busy?" "No, Junior what do you want?" "I need somebody to talk to. I have custody of my son, Trevon, his mom was a caught with drugs in her house. I didn't know she had anything to do with drugs, but I don't know her like that. I was wondering if you would mind if Layla and Malik got to know Trevon. His mom is doing five years." "Where is Shonnie?" "She is still in foster care. Nobody stepped up to take her and I'm not doing it." he said. I laughed to myself. I hoped nobody ever took her.

"Sure, Junior, the kids can meet their brother. You can't bring him here. We can meet at a restaurant or something. It would be best if you called Layla and ask her where she would like to go. You haven't talked to the kids in so long. You should be the one to break the news of them having a brother." "Why can't you do it, Tiffany? You have a better relationship with them." "Do you know why I have I better relationship with them? Because I try, I take the time and get to know them. You should try it, Junior." I said. "Can you put Layla on the phone then?" "Most certainly." I said. Layla got on the phone and talked to her dad for a long while. She made dinner arrangements for the weekend and was excited to meet her new brother.

Malik, on the other hand, was not so forgiving. He was upset his father had another son and he didn't acknowledge him as his son. I had to explain the best I could, his dad still loved him and that's what dads do sometimes. I convinced Malik not to be mad at his dad, and to try to start their relationship over. He said he would for me because I'm the best mommy ever. That made my night. When the weekend finally came, Layla was the only one excited to meet with Junior and Trevon. I wasn't feeling up to sitting around Junior and his love child and neither was Malik.

When we arrived at J. Alexander's in Novi, Layla's favorite place, Junior and Trevon were already seated and waiting on us. We sat down, I watched the interaction between the kids, and it was great. Malik and Trevon looked just alike. Layla on the other hand was a beautiful milk chocolate girl, with long curly hair, her face looked just mine, except for the difference in color. I knew Layla wasn't Junior's daughter, but I wasn't going to say anything. They had a bond and I wasn't about to break it.

Junior asked me if Trevon could spend the night with us, I had to say no because knowing Junior he would take forever to come back and pick this little boy up. The kids wanted him to stay but, I couldn't allow myself to say yes. I liked the little boy, he was smart and spoke well for a three year old. I couldn't bring myself to accept him as Junior's child yet. Only because Angela was his mother. While we thought the kids weren't paying any attention, I asked Junior how he and Angela hooked up.

He told me she came on to him one day while he was watching the kids, he turned her down, but she did it again, he took her up on her offer. He said that shit about him and her getting married was to make me mad. He didn't quite make me mad, but I had to admit it did make me feel some type of way. Trevon kept saying he missed his mom. For a split second, I felt bad, then I went back to not giving a shit.

The dinner was successful for the kids. Layla absolutely loved her dad. He made her promises of coming to get her the next day, I knew he wouldn't. Malik didn't fall for it. He told him if he came he would go but he would not pack his bag until he was at the door. Trevon wanted them to go, with him tonight, which made sense to me as well, but Junior said no he would have to get the house situated. That sounded very peculiar to me. Then Trevon said, "Keisha can get it ready, Daddy."

I told Layla and Malik let's go. I knew it was more going on with Junior and Keisha than what he had told me. I was sick of all of his lies. I didn't have to deal with this shit and I refused to. He tried to stop me to talk to me but, I kept walking like I couldn't hear him. Malik and I went to the car and waited for Layla to come out. When she did she had an attitude. "Why do you have an attitude, Layla?" "Because, now Dad said he's not coming to get us tomorrow." "He was never coming, Layla. How many times have he told you he was coming and didn't? Too many to count right?" "It was going to be different this time, Mom." "What was going to make it different, Puddin' Pop? If he was going to come pick you up tomorrow nothing could stop him, and I mean nothing." Layla was crying. I felt bad but I had to keep it real with her. Both of her parents couldn't lie to her.

The rest of the ride home was quiet until Malik said, "I didn't think he was coming either Layla. He always says the same thing, sometimes he doesn't even talk us for really long time. He doesn't love us like he loves Trevon." "Malik that's not true. He loves you guys all the same. I can't tell you guys why he does the things he does but what I can tell you is that I'm here for you whenever you need me and I promise you that." Layla just continued to cry and Malik smiled. Layla was very sensitive, and like every other girl, she wanted to be loved by her father. I had to do something to cheer her up. "Hey, Puddin' Pop what if we go get some of your friends and I'll take you all to mani's and pedi's? Malik, I'll take you to get a new video game or whatever you want. They both liked that idea.

When we got to the mall, I took Layla and her friends to the nail shop, Malik and I went our way. That's when I saw Michelle and her girls. They saw us and came running over. It had been a long time since I saw Michelle. I wasn't excited to see her. She still seemed depressed. "Hey, Michelle, what's going on?" "Nothing, much. I had to come out to get the girls some shoes. I didn't feel like it." "Are you still having a hard time over your divorce?" I said. "Yes. It's rough." she said. "Why don't you let me take you out for dinner and drinks later today, maybe it'll help you feel a little better." I said. "Nah, I just want to be alone." "Michelle, you have been alone for years. Maybe that's the problem, you don't need to be alone anymore." "No thank you, Tiffany. I'll see you later, I have to get these girls some shoes." she said. I walked away thinking how Michelle could sulk in her own misery for years. Not paying attention to where I was going I bumped straight into Connor.

He was with his wife, Colleen and teenaged daughter, Connie. "Oh my God, I'm so sorry. I wasn't paying any attention to where I was going. Connor Phillips?" I played it off and so did he. "Yes? Do I know you?" "Yes, you sold me my home a while ago. I want to thank you again. My family and I love it." "Oh, yeah I remember you. You are the one who requested the Olympic size swimming pool." "Yep, that's me. Well it was good seeing you and if I know anyone who wants to purchase a home, I'll make sure to send them your way. You're very good at what you do." I said and walked away. I took Malik to get his games and went back to the nail shop to get the girls. They wanted to spend the night, I didn't mind they were good girls, plus it would keep Layla's mind off of Junior's punk ass.

Chapter

8

Later that night, Honey. She was in full swing tonight. She had on a skirt so short, if she sneezed her uterus would be told bless you. I was loving it. I had on a red cat suit it had a plunging neck line. I was showing almost my entire boobs. I looked good. I made me a drink and also one for Honey. I couldn't believe she drunk it and asked for another. As fast as she was drinking them, I was making her more. Before we left my house she was drunk as hell. I drove because I was only buzzed.

When we got to the night club, it was full almost to capacity. As soon as we walked in guys were grabbing all over us. I wasn't ready to find the one I was taking home tonight quite yet. Honey was in the corner grinding with some dude with gold teeth. I laughed at her drunk ass. I kept my eye on her because I knew she wasn't a drinker, I had to see what kind of effect it was having on her. I was on the dance floor having a ball, when Honey came over and asked me if I wanted to go a swingers club with these two fine brothers.

I had no idea what it was, but when I saw who we were going with I said hell yeah. We followed them to this abandoned looking building in the downtown area. I was starting to have second thoughts about this. I felt out of my element. I let Honey talk me into going inside. When we got in there, I was so surprised by what I saw. It was naked people all over the place. It didn't seem to be strange to anybody but me. I felt uncomfortable. I guess the hostess of the party could sense my uneasiness, she came over and talked to me. She told me I didn't have to do anything I didn't want to and there was plenty security if I felt things were getting out of control. She took me around to all the different rooms.

Walking past all the different rooms, seeing all the people having sex or standing around watching, got me aroused. I started to relax. I walked into a room and there was Honey with the two guys we came with. One guy had his dick in her mouth and the other in her pussy. She was taking it like a champ. The guy that had his dick in her mouth, told me to come over to him. I turned him down, I wanted Honey to continue to have her fun. It was plenty men in there I could find to do.

I walked around some more, when a white women stopped me and told me she would like me to be with her and her husband. I hadn't been with a woman before and when I did I wanted to choose her. I walked around and saw this woman, she had a big ass and some nice tits but her man was absolutely gorgeous. I walked up to her and asked her if she would mind if I had sex with her man. She said she was fine with it if she could join in.

I had no problem with that as long as his fine ass would be fucking me. She had on a black sheer negligée.

He man only had on some jeans. He had a six pack and I

wanted to kiss every inch of it. He came over to me and

undressed me. His girl started eating my pussy, I got on my

knees so I could put handsome's dick in my mouth. It was

so small. I was disappointed but I didn't stop. He told his

girl to switch places with him. He ate my pussy while I ate

hers. It wasn't as bad as I thought it would be.

I got up and started sucking on her titties. She was

moaning so sexily, my pussy juices were dripping down my

thighs. I was turned on, I started eating her box again.

When I thought I felt gorgeous enter me from behind, I had

to turn around to make sure. He was, I felt nothing. I guess

his girl could sense my disappointment, she called another

brother over and told him to take care of me while she took

care of her man. We had all had a great time. I had sex with

seven men and four women that night. Honey, on the other

hand said she lost count after the first ten men.

Honey and I went back there the next three weekends in a row. Three times a week, I would see Connor. He was starting to get clingy, I decided I would back off from him. When he noticed me trying to back off, he started sending me flowers and candy at work. I thought it was sweet the first week; however by week three it had become annoying. I told the delivery person to send it back, with a thank you but no thank you note.

He started popping up at my job. I took my job seriously, as a result, I gave in and let him take me out to dinner. "Connor, I think you are getting too attached to me. We had a deal you wouldn't, because you're already married. I'm not looking for a relationship." "Tiffany, I am starting to have feelings for you and you can't fight the feelings you are having for me." "I don't know who told you that I have feelings for you. I like you as a friend but that's all. We have sex like two consenting adults. I have never given you any indications I have any other kind of feelings for you." "When you accept gifts and money from me that's saying we are more than friends and I'm sure you are aware of this, Tiffany." "I thought you were giving me those things because you wanted too." I said.

"Come on Tiff, you're a smart girl. You think I give out $10,000 necklaces and earrings to every woman I have an affair with? Do you think you are the first client I have had an affair with? No, what we did when I sold you your house happens all the time. I have never found anyone as intriguing as you. You get me going in ways my wife can't even do." he said. "Well Connor, it sounds to me like you have yourself a problem. I appreciate the gifts and the money. You are more than welcome to have them back, if you think for one second that means I have feelings for you. On that note, we should cut all ties and this dinner is over. You have a good night Connor." "Tiffany, if you think you can get away from me this easily, you are sadly mistaken. This is far from being over. To be honest with you, with is not over until I say it's over. I know you should get home to your children now, so I'll let you go. Trust me, you will be seeing me soon. Oh, more thing, if I can't have you no one will. Sweet dreams, Tiffany." Connor said.

Connor had me a little scared. I watch a lot of Lifetime movies and from what I get from those, white people are nuts. I tried to stay on Connor's good side until I could figure out what to do with him. I stopped carrying my Beretta with me, I would have to start carrying it again. I thought it was time to have a conversation with Mrs. Colleen Phillips. I knew she could put a stop to Connor's erratic behavior. Most men with money didn't want to lose their wives, it was cheaper and more beneficial to keep them.

I spent the next few months trying not to piss Connor off. I wanted to stay on his good side until I could get up the courage to talk to his wife about the problem. I worked most of the time and spent time with my kids so I could avoid Connor. Any time he felt like it he would show up at my house. I hadn't told my children about him and didn't want them to find out this way. "Connor, I told you not to come to my house. If you wanted to see me we could have made some other arrangements. This is not fair to my children. I don't bring men around them." "I'm not just any man Tiffany. I'm the only man in your life, I don't see anything wrong with me getting to know your children." he said.

"Look, Connor, this is getting out of control. You don't own me, you are not now nor will you ever be the only man in my life. You are married. Doesn't that mean anything to you?" "Not as much as you do, Tiffany. I was thinking about leaving my wife to be with you. I want to make you happy. I can show you I can be the only man you need." "Connor, are you nuts? We don't even know each other that well. I don't have the same feelings as you. What we had was just sex. Nothing more, nothing less." "Tiffany, Tiffany, Tiffany," he said, "You just don't get it do you? How do you think I'm Michigan's top realtor? Because, I go after whatever it is I want and I do whatever it takes to get it. You are no exception. I want you and I'm going to have you, by any means necessary." Connor said. "You sound deranged and I won't tolerate this. Let this be the last time you come here or anywhere else you know I will be. I will filing this with the police and getting a Protective Order against you." I said.

"You don't any proof that I was even here. I haven't done anything out of the ordinary. You have to have a reason to file a Protective Order and as of now you don't have one. I am good at everything I do. I cover my tracks well. I've leave now Tiffany, but you will be seeing me soon." Connor said. He left and I had a funny feeling he was right. I didn't have any proof he was harassing me. He didn't call me, he would just always show up when no one was around. That fucking prick! I had to call his wife soon.

I was out having lunch with Camille, when I spotted Mike across the restaurant. I almost jumped across the table trying to get to him. He was alone. I was apprehensive about approaching him, it had been years since I saw him. I walked over to his table. "Well, lookie here, if it isn't a blast from my past." He looked up at me, smiled and stood. We embraced. "Tiffany, girl how are you? You look great as usual." "Thank you, Mike. You look great as well. It's been so long. How have you been?" I said. "Yes, it has been a long time. I have been good and yourself?" he said.

I've been just fine. Living my life to the fullest. Did you ever get married?" I said. "Yes, I did." "How's your wife?" "She's doing better now. She had cancer, it's been in remission for two years. How's princess Layla?" "She's great. She has a little brother. Actually, two little brothers. One from me and her father and one from the neighbor and her father." "Man, Tiffany, I'm sorry to hear that." "Don't be. Everything happens for a reason. That happened to show me I really didn't need to be with Junior. He still hasn't changed. So, did you ever become that big time lawyer you set out to be?" "Yes, I did. I have been practicing for about four years now and I love it. How about you, did you ever get that college degree you were after?" he said.

"Yes, I have my Master's degree in Healthcare Administration. I am the Research and Development Manager over at Beaumont Hospital. I love it. I'm proud of my accomplishments." "Oh my God, Tiffany that's a great accomplishment and you should be proud, I am." "You have always known what to say and do to make me smile, Mike. It was so nice to see you. I'm having lunch with my friend, but if ever you're in the neighborhood and want to do lunch, here's my business card, call me." I said. "Okay, here is my business card as well. If you ever wanna talk or need a good lawyer give me a call." he said. We hugged and went our separate ways.

When I went back to the table where Camille was sitting she had so much to say. "Who was that, girl?" "That was my old friend, Mike." "I know you hitting that, because he is fine as hell." "No, Honey! He's married. We haven't seen each other in a million years, so it's not like that." "I would definitely make it like that. He looks worth it." "Nah, Camille, I'm not going to even get anything started with Mike. He was my first love and I respect his marriage." I said. We finished lunch and returned to work.

When, I got back to work, I had five messages on my voicemail from Connor. Three of them were saying for me to call him back. Then the more concerning ones started. "I saw you at the restaurant talking to that man. If you want to keep him in that nice package that he's in you'll stay away from him, Tiffany." "Tiffany, I know you got my last messages. If you don't call me back, I will pay a little visit to Mike." he said. I was so sick and tired of Connor I decided now was the time to call his wife.

I called his wife at work. She was an Optometrist. "Hello, this is Dr. Phillips. How may I help you?" Hi, Dr. Phillips, My name is Tiffany Jones and needed to talk with you about a matter that has nothing to do with your business. It's about your husband, I don't know if now is a good time for us to talk or if you would like to meet in person." "If this about you having an affair with Connor, you can tell me something different. I know he told you he wants to leave me to be with you, that's not going to happen. He has an affair almost all the time, so you're not special, dear." she said. "No, Colleen, it's not like that. He has been harassing and stalking me. I did have an affair with him, but I wanted it to end and he doesn't want it to end. I'm calling to see if you could do anything to make him leave me alone." I said.

She laughed so hard at me I started to hang up the phone. "Young lady, there's no way in hell that I believe my husband is obsessed with you. He comes home to me every night. Connor is not a stalker and he doesn't have to harass easy women like you. You women always want more from him. How much money do you want to leave us alone?" "Excuse me? I don't want your money. What I want is for you to get your husband under control. I don't want to have to hurt him; however if he doesn't stop harassing me, I will." "Are you threatening my family?" "No, I'm threatening your husband. I tried to come to you as a woman, but I can see I'm the only woman on this call. Thank you for your time, Dr. Phillips, have a good day." I said and hung up the phone.

I was so upset with myself for trying to reason with a person who was married to a lunatic. Now, I had to take matters into my own hands. I had to upgrade my security system at my home and also my gun. I went to the gun shop and decided on a Glock 30SF. It was a hunting gun, I figured I was being hunted so why not be a hunter as well. I went to the shooting range to sharpen up my skills. I had to watch my back and be prepared for anything.

Chapter

9

So far, it had been a month and I hadn't heard from or seen Connor. This was great, but I still wasn't letting my guard down. I started to do things with Camille again. We had started going back to night clubs. Camille had turned into a really big drinker. I was loving the new change in her. We had so much fun and so much sex with, so many strangers. We had a really bad habit of drinking and driving. I always let Camille drive because I didn't want to mess up my driving record. We had side swiped so many cars. We laughed it off and called the insurance company the next day and pretended like we had no idea what happened.

I was sitting in my office, thinking about Michelle when my phone rang. I hadn't talked to Michelle in three and a half years, she called me out of the blue. "Hey, Tiffie Tiff." said Michelle. "Who is this?" I said. "It's me, Michelle and I'm over Greg and under Chris." she said.

"Well, that's good to hear. Glad you're doing better. To what do I owe this pleasure, Shelly?" I said. "I thought you would be happier to hear from me, Tiffany, damn!" said Michelle. "When I was trying to be happy to hear from you, you didn't want me to be. So, now I'm supposed to jump for joy? I have always tried to be there for you, but you wouldn't let me in. Why should I get all excited now, Michelle?" I said. "I had to do things at my own pace Tiffany. You don't know what's best for everybody. You don't know it all. I was struggling, I was depressed and I was hurt. I loved my husband, unlike you who has no heart and only do things to please yourself." Michelle said.

"I never once said I know it all. What I do know is it shouldn't have taken you over three years to see what I was trying to tell you anyway. I know you can't be that stupid." I said. "I'm not stupid, nor am I Camille. You cannot control my life, like you do hers. We can be on the same level as friends, but I don't need a leader. I'm past trying to be in the "In Crowd". Michelle said. This bitch had some nerves. Who in the fuck did she think she was talking too? I had to teach this bitch a lesson and I had a plan. "Let's meet for lunch." I said.

"Okay, you pick the time and place." Michelle said. "Let's do a late dinner tonight. How about at Andiamo's?" "Tiffany, you know I can't afford to go there." "I didn't ask you if you could afford it. If someone invites you to dinner that means they're paying, Michelle. Be there at 8:30." I said. She said okay and we ended the phone call. I decided to invite Camille too, so we could show Michelle we have fun together. I would lavish her with gifts to win her over.

I went home to start getting ready to meet my friends when all of a sudden, I started to feel sick. I started to feel like I was coming down with the flu. I felt light headed and nauseous. I started to cough. I knew I wasn't pregnant because I was on my period. I called the girls to reschedule the dinner. I took some cold medicine and laid down. In the middle of the night, I started to sweat profusely, my throat and my head was hurting, and my neck was stiff. I knew I was coming down the flu, this was like the worst flu ever.

I stayed at home for a week due to the flu. I felt awful, but when it was over I felt 100% better. I took a lot of over-the-counter medications and it worked like a charm, although I still couldn't shake the cough I had. I returned to work, and was greeted with flowers and cards from my co-workers and Connor. I was surprised to hear from him. How did he know I was sick? I didn't dwell on it too much, I went back to work as usual. I called Camille to see if she would be available for dinner tonight if Michelle was. I still had some unfinished business with Michelle.

"Hey, Camille. How are you?" I said remaining professional because we were at work. She followed suit.

"Hi, Tiffany. I'm fine. I should be asking you that question." "I'm fine now that I'm back at work. That was the worst flu I ever had. I still have a cough but I can deal with that, the other symptoms are what almost took me out." I said laughing. "Anyway Camille, I was calling to see if you are available for dinner tonight, if I can set it up with Michelle?" "Sure. Let me know the details and I'll be there. I missed my friend and I'm glad you're better." she said. "Thanks, Camille. I'll call you with the details. I would say see you at lunch but I'm working through lunch, to try to catch up on some of my work." "Okay, Tiffany, keep me posted." she said.

After the call with Camille, I called Michelle. "Hi, Shelly. How are you?" "I'm good. How are you? I called to check on you a few times, Layla told me you were sleeping but you were doing better." "Yes, I'm much better now. You know as we age are bodies doesn't handle illnesses like they used to. I'm well now and was wondering if you were up for dinner tonight? My treat of course." I said. "Sure. Same place and time?" "The same place, I was thinking we could meet earlier. I want to be home early tonight, so I can help Layla with a project she has for school. I was thinking at like 5:30?" "That's great. I can be home to put the girls to bed." Michelle said. "Okay, Michelle, see you then." I said. I sent Camille an email, giving her the details.

We all met at the restaurant right on time. I ordered drinks for all of us. Michelle was sticking to her 'I don't drink' routine. I convinced her one drink wouldn't kill her. She agreed and drank it. She thought it delicious and ordered another and another. I had to stop her, this time. We all talked and laughed like old times. We had a great time. When we were in the middle of dinner when Connor walked over to the table and asked if he could speak with me. I said no, and kept on talking with my friends. His face turned beet red, he had a hateful look in his eyes. He asked again, and again I said no. He gave me a smirk and turned and walked away.

Michelle was the first to ask what that was all about. I didn't feel like discussing it, I simply said he's a friend and I didn't want to mess up the good time I was having with them to talk to him. I would talk to him later. She okay, but Camille wasn't having it. She knew it was more to it. She didn't inquire at that point, I'm sure she would later. I was wondering how in hell Connor knew I was there or was it coincidental. I had left my Glock at home. I was letting my guard down a little too much. After that I, was ready to go. I told the ladies we would get together again soon, paid the bill and left.

When I got home, I helped Layla with her project and made sure Malik was fine. I decided I would call Connor to get to the bottom of this. This shit was freaking me out. I felt like I didn't have control of this situation and it scared the shit out of me. "Tiffany, my love, I'm glad you decided to call," Connor said, "I thought I was going to have to use drastic measures to get your attention." "Connor, you don't scare me. I wish you would leave me the fuck alone. What is wrong with you?" "I'm in love with you, Tiffany." "Why? I don't have the same feelings for you." "You can learn to love me. I will be a good man to you and a great dad to Layla and Malik. You did a good job helping Layla with her project." he said.

"How did you know that?" I said. "I have my ways, Tiffany. When will you have some time to spend with me? I gave you a break because you were sick, plus you did the stupidest thing when you talked to my wife. She fussed and bitched too much, she was hospitalized for a while, all because of you. You made me hurt Colleen. I didn't want to, but she was talking about hurting you. I couldn't let her do anything to you. I had to show her what would happen to her if she ever thought about it again." "Connor, you are a fucking nutcase. I don't want to have anything to do with you. Stay the fuck away from me and my family. I don't play when it comes to my children. I will kill you with no remorse." I said. "Not if I kill you first." Connor said and hung up.

Chapter

10

That conversation had me really shaken up. I wondered how he knew what was going on in my home. The next day I had an alarm company come out and put up surveillance cameras all around the house, inside and out. They didn't record. That was a feature I didn't think I would need. While the installer was there he found small cameras with microphones connected to them throughout the house. He told me I should get rid of my house phone for a while because it was probably tapped. I couldn't believe Connor had done this. I also had my locks changed on all the doors.

I bet Connor did this to all the houses he sold. He was a true nutcase. When I told Malik, I didn't get the equipment that would record. He told me not to worry he would get it to record. He was very good with technology, so I didn't doubt it. I told him, that if he messed anything up, he would have to get it fixed with his allowance. He agreed and went to work. I never asked if he got it to record. That didn't matter to me. As long as he hadn't messed it up.

I alerted security at work that Connor should not be allowed near my office. I told my secretary I would not except any calls from him. I was feeling really tired and had diarrhea for the last week. I think my nerves were getting the best of me. I continued to work through my fatigue. If I wasn't working I was sleeping. I was having horrible night sweats and I was starting to lose weight. I had to stop letting Connor stress me out.

I hadn't heard from Connor in over three months and I was happy as hell. I didn't think he was out of the picture, I think he was waiting for me to let my guard down. He would have a long wait because I would forever be on guard. Camille, Michelle and I had been hanging out together. Michelle was still a prude. It was time to put my plan into action. I went to visit my friend in the city, who

sold any kind of drug you could think of. I purchased about

twenty ecstasy pills and some cocaine. I would make

Michelle a concoction I heard people talking about. I

planned a girl's get away for a week.

I booked me and girls round trip tickets to Las Vegas. I

booked us a suite at the Bellagio Hotel on Las Vegas

Boulevard. They both were so excited. I left Layla and

Malik at their friend's house for the week. It was summer

vacation and they would have been there most of the time

anyway. We went shopping, I didn't have any clothes that

fit anymore. I had lost 45 lbs. in three months. I was now

wearing a size 8. I looked very thin and frail, but to me I

still looked good. Camille was the first to make a comment

about it. "Damn, Tiffany, what kind of weight loss program

are you on?" "Stress." I said. "It doesn't seem like you

have anything to stress about. I wish I had your life."

Michelle said. "Trust me, Shelly, you don't want my life. Don't forget I have a stalker. That's why my ass has lost all this weight. Let's finish shopping bitches, we're leaving tomorrow." I said.

I told Camille and Michelle to stay the night at my house, I have a car picking us up to take us to the airport. Camille was all for it, but of course, Michelle had to be difficult. "Why can't you have the car come to my house and pick me up, you have to pass by here to get to the airport." "Because that's not the way I want to do it, Michelle. If we are all together, we won't be late." "Okay then, let's stay at my house then. I have enough room." "No, Michelle, we are going to stay at my house and that is final. If not, find your own way to the airport and don't be late because I have your ticket." "Fine, Tiffany. I will find my own way." Michelle said.

The next day, Camille and I made it to the airport two hours before our plane was scheduled to leave. I walked to one of the shops to get some magazines, when I thought I saw Connor. I looked again and the person was gone. I must have been tripping, it's no way he would have known I was at the airport. I bought my magazines and went back to where Camille was. Michelle had finally made it. "I thought I saw Connor. He disappeared so fast I can't be sure." I said.

"We will keep our eye out for him. Don't worry girl. We're going to Vegas to get away from our troubles." Camille said. "Yeah, Tiff. We got your back." Michelle said. "He's crazy, you guys. I don't underestimate him. I don't have my gun, so I can't shoot that son of a bitch. We're from the D, we will show his ass what's up. I'm sick of him playing with me." I said. "I know that's right." They both said in unison. We joked around until it was time for us to board the plane. We had a ball on the plane. I still kept my eye out for Connor.

We got to the hotel, it was absolutely gorgeous. We rushed up to our suite, got cleaned up, put on our swimming suits and lounged by the pool. It was beautiful in Las Vegas. We couldn't wait until it got dark and we could see what the night life was like. I called and made a reservation for a rental car. They were delivering it to our hotel in a few hours. We were going sightseeing and out for dinner and drinks.

I was starting to feel sick. My throat and head was starting to hurt. My cough hadn't completely left since I had the flu months ago. I went to the room and took some of the flu medicine I brought with me. It made me sleepy, so I told the girls I was going to take a nap for a while. I was asleep for three hours, Michelle woke me up because I was sweating profusely. She felt my head and I had a fever.

She ran down to the hotel store and got me some Tylenol. I took it and assured her I was would be fine in a few hours, I was jet lagged. I didn't know why I felt like this all the time, but I didn't want to spoil our trip worrying about it.

I woke up to the phone ringing. It was the front desk telling me the rental car was being delivered. I got up, still feeling sick and went down to sign for it. I must have really been sick because I was hallucinating. I thought I saw Connor staring at me from across the street. I had to be drugged from the medication I had taken. I went back up stairs and took a long hot bath. I was starting to feel a little better. Camille and Michelle came in and were pleasantly surprised to see me up and in the bath. They had been walking around sightseeing. I got out the bath and got dressed.

I told them I was playing bartender while we were on vacation, they agreed. Michelle said she would only have wine. I told her she would have whatever the bartender decided to make. She was hesitant. I told her to just relax and have fun this week. She got on my fucking nerves always acting so politically correct. I made us Passion Fruit Mojitos. I crunched up two ecstasy pills and added a little cocaine to Michelle's first one. She really enjoyed it. The next few she had were regular. She was totally different person. Camille asked me what was wrong with her. I told her that she was acting crazy because she wasn't a real drinker. She believed me.

We went to dinner at Sushi Roku's in Caesars Palace. The restaurant was breathtaking and the food was delicious. We enjoyed more drinks and decided to go The Gold Boutique Night Club and Lounge. It was a nice crowd for a Wednesday night. The three of us were on the dance floor all night. We had an excellent time. To end the night I needed to find some dick. I scanned the room and didn't see anybody worth my time. It was our first night there so I wasn't that pressed. We stayed until the club closed.

We got back to the hotel and had to carry Michelle to the room. I felt guilty for drugging her for about two seconds, then I felt empowered. This bitch doesn't know I am the leader of this little clique. We put her high ass to bed and decided to sit out on our balcony and watch the night life. I couldn't believe it was after 4 a.m. and the streets were still full of people. I was starting to love Las Vegas.

We did the same thing every night. I continued to drug Michelle. She was asking me to make her drinks as soon as we woke up in the morning. It was my pleasure. I had to slow down I was running out of the concoction. Our last night there, I was standing on the balcony with a drink in my hand, when I looked down I was sure as hell I saw Connor staring straight up at me. I called Camille out on the balcony so she could tell me if I was going crazy. She saw him too. He walked away and blended into the crowd, we lost sight of him. I was scared shitless. I wanted to go home. The girls didn't want to go. Camille said we would be extra cautious. I told them I was staying in. They convinced me to go, saying it was easier for him to get to me if I was in a hotel room by myself. That made sense. I wasn't going to let Connor mess up my last night in Vegas.

I made Michelle two really strong concocted drink. She drank one down in one gulp but the other one Camille picked up and downed in one gulp. I almost shitted on myself. I didn't want Camille to have any of that shit, but fuck it, what could I do about it now. We got dressed and went to another club. This club was across the city. Since the two bitches with me were high and drunk I had to drive. I hated to drive. We got to the club and had a ball. They were so drunk they could barely stand up. I didn't care, I was talking to a fine brother, who was saying all the right shit to get in my pants.

He wanted me to go back to his room with him. Since we had been out of town I had only slept with one guy and my body needed to be loved. I told the two drunk asses I was leaving with the dude and gave them the keys to the car. At first I didn't think it was a good idea to let them drive because they were so drunk, but Camille and I had done it a million times before, she would be fine. I left with the fine brother, whose name I didn't care to know.

I had a remarkable time with him. His sex game was the bomb and I appreciated it so much. It was a welcomed departing gift. I made it back to the hotel at 6 a.m. There were no signs of Camille or Michelle. I went to bed. They probably found somebody and went back to their rooms. I was sleeping for three hours when there was a loud knock on the door. I was going to kill these bitches for not having their room keys. I opened the door and it was two police officers. If those dumb asses were in jail for drunk driving they were going to stay. "Tiffany Jones?" the older officer said. "Yes?" "Did you know Camille Rodgers and Michelle Turner?" "What do mean you did? Yes, I know them. They are not here right now, but if you tell me what this concerning I will have them contact you as soon as they get in." "Ma'am, I'm sorry to inform you, but your friends were killed in a car accident early this morning. We need you to come and identify their bodies." the younger officer said.

Chapter

11

My body went numb and I fainted. When I woke up I was in the hospital. I thought I had a bad dream. I pushed the button for the nurse. She came in with a sad look on her face. Right then I knew it wasn't a dream, my friends were dead. I started to cry. She told me the doctor needed to talk to me. The doctor came in, I thought he was about to talk to me about Camille and Michelle. The next thing he said to me made me faint again. He told me I was HIV positive. I couldn't believe it. I didn't think people like me could get a deadly disease like this.

I didn't think this could happen to me. This was too much for me to handle. The police officers walked in. They came to tell me although, Camille's alcohol level was over the legal limit that was not what killed them. The brake line on the car had been cut. They were asking me question after question, it was like they were speaking a different language, and I could not understand what they were saying. They took me down to the morgue to identify the bodies. The girls were bruised and had a few scratches but they looked like they were sleeping. I broke down crying again. One of the officers helped me back to my room.

This was too much to digest. I had to tell both of their families. I didn't know how I would tell them. I couldn't get the words out so the nurse took the phone and did it for me. I had to be strong, I still had to go to the police station and answer more questions. For once in my life I was truly sad. It was like my heart was broken. I loved my girls, especially Camille. She was my best friend, my partner in crime. I had known Michelle my entire life. Now these women were gone. I would never see their faces again. I got dressed and went to the police station.

I talked to a detective, who was interested in knowing who would cut the brake line on the car. The first person that came to my mind was Connor. I told the detective the entire story about Connor and me. I also told him Camille and I saw him staring up at us while we were on the balcony. He made some phone calls and could not confirm that Connor was in Nevada or had been at all that week. I was pissed. They let me go and I made arrangements for the girls' bodies to flown back to Michigan. That was the hardest thing I ever had to do.

I took the next available flight home. I was having flu like symptoms again, but this time I knew they were associated with HIV. The entire flight I analyzed my life and the stupid decisions I made. I guess this is what regret feels like because I regretted everything I had done. I had done awful things to people and didn't care. Now all of it was coming back to haunt me. My two friend's children would never see them again, because I wanted to control their lives, when I really didn't even have control of my own. I wish I had made better decisions. I was out having unprotected sex because I wanted too. More than half of the men I slept with I didn't know their names. I had no idea when or where I contracted the virus. This was another selfish decision I made. What about my own children?

My plane landed, I didn't want to get off. I wanted to continue to fly until I woke up from this nightmare, but I had to face reality. When I got home the first thing, I did was go pick up Layla and Malik. I told them about Camille and Michelle and they were instantly saddened. Then Layla said something that made me slap her. "It's a sad situation, but better them than you." "Don't you ever say that shit, again. Those women were my friends and they have kids that love them as much as you love me." "Sorry, mommy, but I'm glad you weren't in the car. I'd rather go their funeral than yours." "Layla, I don't like your outlook on this and I don't want to talk about it with you anymore." I said. I was baffled, I couldn't believe how little regard she had for the people in this horrific situation.

It was hard dealing with both Camille and Michelle's grieving families. They blamed me. They wanted me to be in the car too. I paid for their funerals, I felt it was the least I could do. The funerals were so sad. I cried for weeks. I cried not only for the pain of losing my friends but for everything that ever pained me in my life. I called Mike, I needed to be comforted and do some good for once in my life. When I called his office they told me that he was off due to a family emergency. I called his cell phone, he answered. "Hey, Mike. How are you? Is now a good time for you to talk, I really need a friend." "Yes, now is as good as any. I need a friend too. I'm so happy that you called. It's like you read my mind." he said. That was the comfort I was looking for. "It's good to hear you say that, Mike. I have so much going on in my life I swear I want to kill myself." "Tiffany, please don't say stuff like that. Whatever you're going through can't be all that bad." he said. I explained everything I was going through, except the part about me having HIV. He didn't say a word he listened until I finished.

"Wow, you are going through a lot. My wife's cancer came back with a vengeance. She's in the hospital. She refuses to get treatment, the only thing she will take is medication for pain. It hurts so badly. She's being so selfish, but at the same time, I understand. I understand she doesn't want to be cut anymore, or go through chemo, but what am I supposed to do? Sit back and watch her die?" "Yes, Mike you are. You are supposed to be supportive. Help her through this. This can't be an easy decision for her. She has thought about you and she knows you will be fine." "How am I supposed to support her killing herself?" "She's not killing herself, Mike. Cancer is killing her.

Cancer is not something you can catch from another person or people stand in line to get, it just happens. It's not her fault nor is it yours. If it is anything I can do for you, please let me know. You will need someone to help you get through this. I can get you some help from someone at the hospital if you want me too." I said.

"I love the woman you have become, Tiffany. Thank you so much. I'll take you up on your offer. I will help you with the problem we talked about. I know a judge, he owes me a favor. We both will get through our problems. If you don't mind, I would like to stay in constant contact with you. I feel better when I talk to you." "Of course, Mike. I would like that a lot." "Okay, I spend most of my time at the hospital, when you get back to work, let's do lunch." "I would really like that. I'm going back to work really soon. Hopefully, I'll see you soon." I said and we hung up the phone. I had work to do to start putting my life back in order.

I made myself an appointment to see a doctor that specializes in HIV and women's health. I had done research on HIV, it's more complex in women, so finding a doctor who realizes in the special challenges of women with the disease, was important to me. I found a doctor named Kimberly Potter. She got me in almost immediately. I was nervous and scared of what she and her office staff would think of me.

When I entered the office, it was two other female patients in there. They didn't look like they had HIV, but neither did I. The office staff was courteous and very kind. I started to relax. When I went to the back to have the series of test done, I was nervous about the results, like I didn't already know them. When the test came back positive I cried all over again. I was tired of crying. I did this to myself, it was time I started to take responsibility for this. I stopped crying and the doctor started talking to me. "Tiffany, it's not the end of your life. There are medications that can prolong life. You can still live life, cautiously, but you can live. Do you know who gave you the disease?" "No, I have no idea. I'm not blaming anybody for this, but me. I was never taught to use protection other than birth control, the biggest thing was to not get pregnant. I am an educated woman, I knew better than the behavior I was exhibiting, but I didn't care. I thought this was a disease for crack heads or prostitutes, not wealthy educated women like me." I said.

"Lately, I have been proving myself to be wrong about almost everything I have done in my life. Karma is really a bitch." I said. "We all make mistakes, Tiffany. The best part is you are still in the primary stage which means the medications will work better for you. I think maybe you should join a support group for women with HIV. It would be very beneficial to you. You will see you are not alone." Dr. Potter said. We talked a while longer, she gave me my prescriptions and told me start taking them as soon as I got them. I went to the pharmacy far from my house, I was embarrassed of the medications I was getting. The next thing I did was made a phone call to Junior.

"Hey, Junior how you been?" "I've been fine. How are you? I heard about what happened in Vegas. Sorry for your lost." "Thank You. I calling because I want you to be in Layla and Malik's life. I should say I need you to be in their lives." "You sound like your dying or something, Tiff." he said laughing. "Well, Junior, I might be. I haven't shared this information with anyone else and would like for you to keep it between us. Can you do that for me?" "Of course. What's wrong?" "While I was in Las Vegas I found out I have HIV." I said. There was silence on the phone. I was quiet too, giving Junior his time to process what I said.

"You have to be kidding me, right?" "I wish I was, Junior. The doctor said it's in the primary stages and with medication, I should live long, but I'm not too hopeful about this situation. You should get tested, Junior. I'm not sure when I contracted this, so get tested to be on the safe side."

"I know you didn't give me that nasty ass disease, girl. If I had it I would look like had it or I would have some symptoms." "Junior, I thought the same thing. That's not true. There is no look. Symptoms can be simple and you might think it's something else. Some people have no symptoms for years. I think you should tested. That doesn't mean you have it. For the kids' sake, I think it's better to know than not to know. Please, do it for them." "Okay, Tiff, but we haven't had sex in such a long time I'm sure I didn't catch it." "Have you always had protected sex, both oral and intercourse?" "No." "Get tested, Junior." I said. He promised he would. He also said he would start coming around the kids and he did. Layla and Malik even liked Angela.

She got out of prison early, when the evidence in her case disappeared, thanks to Mike. Junior and Angela were in a relationship. I was genuinely happy for them. Mike's wife's passed, soon after I secretly became Tiffany Jones-Robinson, but we weren't ready to tell anyone quite yet. Mike, Junior, and Angela were all tested for HIV and the three of them were negative. I was relieved. Things in my life were going great. My kids loved Mike and so did I. My life was finally shaping up. I talked to my mother and brothers. We were talking about visiting each other soon. I was finally happy. I started going to a support group for women living with HIV. It was very helpful. I learned people from all walks of life did have the disease.

Having protected sex was no different from having unprotected sex. Mike and I had a really healthy sex life. I always made sure we were very safe. I didn't want to risk him catching what I had. As I was leaving for a meeting one night, I stepped outside, right into Connor's face. He grabbed me by the arm and pushed me into his car. "If you scream, I will kill you in front of your children." "Where are you taking me, Connor?" "Shut the fuck up, Tiffany. You know, I have really grown to hate you. You are the only person you think about. You made me kill your friends. If you would have driven the car your fucking self, instead of being a whore and going off fucking some guy you didn't know, all this would be over. I told you if I can't have you, nobody will." "Connor, I was getting everything out of my system before I settled down with you. I had all intentions on being with you." "Bitch, who do you think I am? You cannot tell me anything and think I'm going to

185

believe it." he said. He hit me over the head with a flashlight and I blacked out.

When I woke up I had no idea where I was. It was dark and smelled like gas. I assumed I was in a garage or warehouse. I tried to move and noticed I was tied up. I decided to give up and face my destiny. I'd done so much wrong to people, I deserved this. I wanted death to hurry up and come to me, then I thought about Mike, Layla, and Malik. My three reasons for living. I started to fidget around trying to see if I could get my hands loose. The ropes were burning my wrist but I didn't give a shit, I kept at it. They weren't getting loose and I was getting tired.

I heard a noise and played like I was still unconscious. A light came on, I opened my eyes to take a quick look. I was in Connor's garage, his car was inside, also. I needed to get to my purse and my Glock. Connor walked over to me and smacked me, trying to wake me up. I opened my eyes. He untied me, and told me to get undressed. I paused, he yelled at me and told me to undress. I did as I was told. If he was going to kill me, why not give him something that would eventually kill him and his wife.

After I got undressed, he pulled his pants down and told me not to resist or I would never see my family again. I didn't resist, I didn't even want to. I let me take me how he wanted me. He was the only man I had ever used a condom with and it was his choice. I guess the only thing he was worried about was getting me pregnant. As soon as he was finished, we heard someone calling his name. He hurriedly put his pants on. "Don't you say one word or you will watch your children die tonight." he said through gritted teeth. He turned off the light and rushed into the house. I heard the door close and conversation start, I ran over to his car and grabbed my purse. I put my clothes back on and waited for him to come out the door.

The minute the door opened. I shot two shots towards the door. I heard a body fall to the ground. I got up off the floor and turned the light on. I looked down at the body and almost lost my mind. It wasn't Connor I shot it was his teenaged daughter, Connie. I heard footsteps then screaming. "Oh my God, Connie. Connor call 9-1-1. Please hurry." Colleen said. I heard Connor calling 9-1-1. I was crouching in a corner when he entered the garage.

He ran to the corner and grabbed me. I was almost hysterical. "What did you do, Tiffany? What the fuck did you do?" Connor said through tears. Colleen ran over toward me and spit in my face. That's when the police and ambulance arrived. They told the police I was an intruder. I was automatically arrested and booked with first degree murder. I never had a chance to tell my side of the story. I was a black woman who killed a teenaged white girl in her home. They didn't want to hear me. I was told I would be serving a life sentence. This would be my second life

sentence. HIV was my first.

To be continued......

This story was fun to write because I like being creative and being able to use my imagination. HIV is not imaginative. It's real. 1 in 6 people have HIV and are unaware of it. 1 in 4 new cases are in the 13-24 age group. African Americans are the race that is most burdened with the disease. In 2010, African American heterosexual women were in the top cases. Although, African American only make up 14% of the population of the United States population, we accounted for 44% of the new HIV infection cases in 2010. This shit is real. I get tested once a year because, I want to know. I don't want to be a statistic. This disease is preventable. Have protected sex and please get tested. It's painless and it only takes a few seconds. Also, I do not promote drinking and driving. Drunk drivers takes over 10,500 lives in the United State and injures over 345,000 per year. Most drunk drivers are repeat offenders.

Do not drink and drive. The life you save might be your

own. If you want more statistics click the link below:

http://aids.gov/hiv-aids-basics/hiv-aids-101/statistics//

http://www.madd.org/statistics/